Message in a Bottle

A NOVELLA

BETH WISEMAN

Message In A Bottle

Copyright 2016 Beth Wiseman
Published by Beth Wiseman in Fayetteville, Texas

Cover design: Beth Wiseman
Interior design: Caitlin Greer

ISBN-13: 978-0-9976610-0-2

To Audrey Wick

Prologue

Kyle stretched tape across another box, then lifted it from the floor and piled it on top of the others that he had ready to go.

"I can't believe all this stuff was stashed in this small room." Lexie lowered a stack of file folders into a box. "I don't think I had nearly this much in my dorm room." She grinned as she slung long brown hair over her shoulders. "And I'm a girl. We keep everything."

Kyle eyed the organized mess in the place he'd called home over the past four years. "Some of it probably needs to be trashed, but I'll take a closer look at everything once I get settled in my apartment." He handed Lexie the tape. "Just think, you'll be right downstairs from me. No curfews or rules. We can eat pizza at three in the morning, and we won't have to deal with crazy roommates."

Lexie closed the distance between them and pressed her soft lips gently against his. Kyle eased his arms around her and basked in the scent of her flowery perfume. The feel of her mouth on his was a welcome distraction. They'd briefly considered moving in together, but Kyle's Catholic upbringing kept him from choosing that option. They'd done the next best thing: rented apartments close to each other.

"Maybe we should take a break from packing," Kyle whispered in her ear, trailing kisses down her neck.

She wiggled out of his arms. "Behave. We've got to get this done. You've got to be out of here by the end of the day." She walked to the built-in drawers in Kyle's room and tugged the bottom one until it inched open. "Good grief. What is all this?"

Kyle shuffled across the floor in his socks until he was beside her and staring at the massive amount of pictures, ticket stubs, receipts, and other memorabilia crammed in the top drawer. Sighing, he thumbed his way through the first layer. "Keepsakes."

Lexie smiled as she picked up a picture. "Awe, look at you and Aiden. So handsome."

"My mom sent me that the first week I was here, along with a bunch of other pictures." Kyle recalled how homesick he was at that time. "I was probably seventeen in that picture. Aiden was sixteen."

"Baseball players, I see." Lexie brought the photo closer to her face. "You and your brother look a lot alike in this picture, but not so much in person." She reached for a ticket stub that was folded in half and straightened it. Kyle rolled his eyes as she burst out laughing. "Lady Gaga?"

Kyle shrugged as his mind flooded with memories. "Yeah, well. I wasn't the one who wanted to go see her, but she actually put on a great show."

"Was this your date?" Lexie held up a photo that was right underneath the ticket. Kyle had his arm around the first girl he'd ever loved. Morgan Calhoun. And thoughts of her still caused his heart to race, even though he was sure no one could be in love as much as he and Lexie. There was no doubt in his mind that he'd marry Lexie one day.

"Yeah. That's Morgan." He swallowed hard. "We grew up on the same street, our families went to the same church, and our moms were best friends." He forced a smile. "My first—and only love—before you."

"Kyle Brossmann, do you expect me to believe that there have only been two loves in your life?"

The question made Kyle wonder how many loves had been in Lexie's life, but it really didn't matter. He'd be the one blessed to live with her for the rest of his days. He hoped.

Kyle nodded. "Yep. There was Morgan. And now you." He eased the photo from her hand and studied Morgan's face, the way her blonde hair curled under slightly below her chin, then tapered past her shoulders. She had magnificent brown eyes and a smile that made people like her before she ever uttered a word. And a body that made guys go nuts. Kyle had questioned her interest in him from day one, knowing someone as attractive as Morgan could have dated anyone she wanted.

"She's really pretty. I'm surprised you haven't mentioned her before." Lexie put her head on his shoulder. "How long did you two date?"

Kyle tucked his dark hair behind his ears, knowing he'd have to shed his long locks before he started his new job. "We dated about a year, but we sort of grew into it. Since we'd known each other most of our lives, we were friends way before anything else." He set the picture back in the drawer, forcing thoughts of Morgan away. Five years later, it was still painful to think about her. But Lexie had already found another selfie of Morgan and Kyle at the beach, the murky Gulf of Mexico in the background. Kyle remembered the cloudy day in Galveston. They'd eaten at Shrimp 'N Stuff and walked on the beach. Kyle looked like his face was twice as big as it really was in the picture. But Morgan looked perfect in her pink bikini top and freshly applied lip gloss.

Lexie couldn't seem to pull her eyes away from the photo. That's the affect Morgan had on most people.

"So what happened with you two?"

It was a conversation Kyle didn't want to have, but if he was going to marry Lexie some day, he supposed there shouldn't be any secrets. "It's a crazy story."

Lexie nudged him gently with her elbow, grinning. "I love crazy stories."

Kyle took a deep breath as all the memories he'd fought to suppress came rushing to the surface. He lowered himself to the edge of the mattress, perching on the corner as he began. "Back in high school, I pulled up to Morgan's house in my truck and honked the horn. She rode with me to school every day, even though she had her own car. I waited, honked again, waited some more, then finally went to the front door and knocked. No answer." His heart hammered against his chest, but he figured he might as well get this over with, then he'd pack up his memories for good. Seal them tight with extra tape, keepsakes his grandchildren would find some day and ask, "Who is this woman grandpa is with?" From heaven, he'd whisper, "My first love."

"Then what?" Lexie eased her way to the bed and sat down.

"I looked in the window, and through the sheer drapes, I could see that the living room was empty. I mean, totally empty. No furniture. Nothing." Kyle felt the sweat beads pooling on his forehead, much like five years ago. "I opened the front door, which was unlocked, and I went through the whole house yelling Morgan's name." He turned to face Lexie, pushed the drawer shut with the heel of one foot, then leaned against the dresser. "There was not one piece of furniture in that entire house."

"I'm confused." Lexie tipped her head to one side, frowning. "Did Morgan and her family just pack up in the middle of the night and disappear?"

Kyle tried to calm the churning in his stomach. "That's exactly what happened."

"Where'd they go?"

"No one knows. It was totally bizarre. My mom was devastated. Maybe even more than me. Morgan's mom and my mom had been pregnant at the same time with us, and they'd been best friends long before Morgan or I could even walk. Mom even hired a private detective to try to find them, convinced that some sort of kidnapping or evil was at work. But the guy took Mom's money and never came up with one single clue."

"Wow." Lexie leaned back on the palms of her hands and blew out a big burst of air she'd been holding. "That *is* a crazy story. I bet that's really haunted you over the years."

You have no idea how much. "Yeah, it did." He walked to the bed, sat down beside her, and leaned in for a kiss. "But I have you. And wherever Morgan is, I hope she's well. But she's a part of my past. My future is with you."

But even as Kyle said the words, his thoughts and memories swam in his head like hungry sharks, wondering about Morgan. Where is she now? Is she happy? Did she go to college like they'd planned to do together?

Where are you, Morgan?

Chapter One

One year later…

Morgan sat in a chair by the hospital bed waiting for Emma to wake up. She always woke up, thank God. The medicines knocked her out, but she wasn't going to drift away in her sleep. Not today anyway.

"The guys left about three hours ago," her father said in a whisper as he walked into the room, gently closing the door behind him.

Morgan didn't turn around. She recognized her father well before she got a visual of him. Neal Calhoun had worn the same musky cologne Morgan's entire life. "I know."

She slumped into the chair as she watched her baby girl sleeping. Emma was five. Not really a baby. But curled in a fetal position on her side, and at six pounds lighter than when they'd arrived at the hospital, she looked like a tiny baby to Morgan.

Her father picked up a chair from the other side of the room and tiptoed to where Morgan was. He gently set the chair down and eased into it. "How's our girl today?"

"She's good." Morgan answered for her daughter since the medicine had made her drowsy. "The doctor was in earlier, and if she stays on this course the rest of the day, she can go home." Morgan reached for a cup of water on the nightstand.

Her father nodded to the lounging chair in the far corner. "Were you able to get some sleep during the night?"

Morgan finished sipping from the cup of water and put it back. "Yeah. As well as anyone can sleep in a hospital, I guess."

They were quiet for a few moments, both watching the rise and fall of Emma's chest as she slept. Morgan's dad crossed one leg over the other and gently kicked it into motion. Her father was a man trained not to show any sort of nervousness, but when it came to his daughter and granddaughter, he was as ineffective as a sheer curtain trying to block out ultraviolet rays.

She reached into her purse and pulled out a bottle of ibuprofen, popped two in her mouth, and chased them back with another swig of water. She stared into the almost empty bottle and thought about all the little notes she used to leave for Kyle on Fridays after school. It felt like a lifetime ago. He'd had an irregular heartbeat and took a pill for it every morning on the way to school after he had picked her up. After swallowing it without any water, he would toss the bottle in the console of his Chevy Silverado. On Fridays she'd sneak out to his truck and leave him a note inside the bottle, knowing he'd find it Saturday morning on the way to work. "Messages in a bottle" he'd tell her.

Emma coughed and both Morgan and her father watched and waited, but Emma stayed asleep. "She looks so much better," Morgan said to her father.

Dad shifted his weight in the chair, his foot still moving nervously back and forth. He finally uncrossed his legs, but he kept a slow steady tap of one shoe going. "Everything is going to be okay," he said softly.

Morgan was quiet for a few moments. "What if he doesn't come?"

"He'll come."

Dad was a man used to getting his way. He loved God and he loved his family, but his desire to protect and provide sometimes crossed so many lines that Morgan felt like she stayed on a tightrope, striving to maintain balance somehow.

"It's been almost six years. What if he's married? Gone? Doesn't care?" That last part didn't sound like Kyle, but people change. Morgan sure had.

She glanced at her father when she felt his gaze on her. She raised an eyebrow and reminded herself who she was dealing with. As a CIA agent, her father would know everything there is to know about Kyle.

"I told you, he's not married."

Morgan took a deep breath. "But you said he's planning on getting married."

"Not for a few months, according to my source."

Morgan's father never revealed his sources, and most of the time, Morgan was sure that was a blessing. Her heart grew heavy as she thought about Kyle marrying someone else. But then, why shouldn't he? Her family had surely knocked the breath from his lungs the day they'd packed up and left in the middle of the night. But her former love had obviously moved on and was planning a future with someone else. *As it should be.*

But oh...how she'd love to be a fly on the wall when Landon and Sean showed up at Kyle's door.

Kyle awoke to the smell of bacon sizzling and coffee brewing. He stretched, yawned, and sat up in bed, knowing Lexie was busy in his kitchen. She did that most Saturdays, used her key, snuck in, and started breakfast. She'd arranged the kitchen in Kyle's apartment the way she liked it, knowing it would be her kitchen in a few months. Kyle was ready. Lexie was the love of his life, everything he'd ever wanted in a spouse and soul mate.

"Good morning, sleepyhead." She walked into the bedroom and handed him a cup of coffee.

"You spoil me," he said before he took a sip.

"You deserve to be spoiled." Lexie sat down on the side of his bed, smiling, and in full makeup.

"Where are you off to so early?" Kyle ran a hand through his short hair, not more than a couple of inches on the top and closely shaved on each side.

"I'm picking up Mom, and we're heading to a little boutique on the other side of Houston." Lexie rolled her eyes, grinning. "I'm starting to wonder if she'll ever find a dress for the wedding." She nodded toward the opened bedroom door. "I made you breakfast, but I already ate so I can get on the road."

Lexie's parents lived about forty-five minutes from the complex where Kyle and Lexie each had an apartment. Soon, there would be a merger into just Kyle's apartment, and not only could Kyle not wait to wake up next to Lexie every morning, they'd also be able to sock away some money by having just one rent to pay.

She leaned down and kissed him, grimacing.

"You should know better than to do that before I brush my teeth." He set the cup down and pulled her to him anyway, smothering her with kisses as she faked a struggle.

"Ewe, yuck, mister." She giggled as she finally freed herself. "Get your lazy butt up and brush those teeth." Blowing him a kiss, she turned at the door of his bedroom when he said her name. "Yeah?"

Kyle sat up in bed and stared at her. He didn't think she'd changed at all over the two years since he'd first met her, except she'd grown even more beautiful, if that was possible. "Do you have any idea how much I love you?"

She playfully tapped a finger to her chin, lifting an eyebrow as she pushed long strands of hair away from her face. "Hmm... I believe you said you love me with all your heart."

Kyle smiled. *I am a blessed man.* "With all my heart, to the moon and back."

She blew him another kiss and left.

Kyle shuffled to the kitchen, ate two pancakes and some bacon, then decided more sleep was in order on this rainy Saturday. Houston was hot in June. Throw in some rain, and it was miserably muggy. He awoke an hour later when someone banged on the door.

"Coming!" He slipped into a pair of jeans he'd left on the floor the night before, and he pulled a black ZZ Top T-shirt over his head on the way to see who it was. Looking through the peep hole, he saw two tall—and large—men. One of the guys looked to be about Kyle's age or a little older, and he wore a dark suit. The other man was considerably older and

13

wore tan slacks and a yellow Polo shirt. "Yeah, what is it?" he yelled through the door.

"Kyle Brossmann? We need to talk to you. Can we come in?" the older guy asked. When Kyle didn't answer, the same man held up a… *badge?* Kyle closed one eye and squinted with the other until he could read the small print. *Central Intelligence Agency.*

Kyle's heart thudded so hard against his chest he feared he might have a heart attack at his young age. Recently, he'd gotten a speeding ticket. He'd sped through the toll booth without paying too. He'd paid his Visa credit card two days late. He'd cut the tag off a new pillow even though it warned not to.

His head was reeling, but he couldn't think of anything to warrant the CIA at his door. *Lexie.* Had something happened to her? *But the CIA doesn't show up to report an accident.*

"Uh, what can I help you with?" he managed to say loudly.

"Mr. Brossmann, we just need a few minutes of your time. Can you open the door?" Now the young guy was talking, but while Kyle was still pondering what to do, the older man held his identification even closer to the peep hole.

These guys aren't going away. Kyle opened the door. "Yeah?"

"We're sorry to bother you so early, but it's important we talk to you," the older guy said.

Kyle glanced at his watch. It wasn't so early. Ten o'clock. But he held his position.

The younger of the two men cleared his throat. "We need to talk to you about Morgan Calhoun."

Kyle's heart pounded like a jack pump in an oilfield. "What about her? Is she hurt or something?" *Or dead.* Adrenaline coursed through his veins, winding and weaving and causing havoc at every nerve ending in his body. Why else would the CIA show up at your door unless there had been a death, a murder, or something equally as awful? He stepped aside so the men could come in, each one stowing an umbrella by the front door. "Where is she?" It was the question Kyle had put to rest years ago, deciding it was a mystery that would never be solved.

"Morgan's fine." The older man extended his hand. "I'm Sean, and this is Landon."

Morgan is okay. Relief washed over Kyle in a wave of emotion that threatened to knock him off his feet. He latched on to Sean's hand, wondering if these guys had last names, and hoping he would get some answers after all these years.

Sean pointed to the couch. "Can we sit and talk for a few minutes?"

Kyle nodded. He was pretty sure he wasn't supposed to argue with the CIA.

Sean and Landon sat on the couch. Kyle found the edge of a recliner nearby, although he sat straight and rigid, barely breathing. Sean had thinning gray hair and dark eyes. The other guy—Landon—had wavy blond hair, a dark tan, and blue eyes. But they had one thing in common. They were both huge. And not in a bad sort of way, but muscular and thick.

"Where's Morgan?" Kyle asked again.

Sean glanced at Landon, then back at Kyle. "This is going to be a little shocking, but… "

"What?" Kyle asked in barely a whisper, hoping they didn't see his bottom lip trembling like it had a mind of its own.

"It's really more about Emma," Landon said.

"Who's Emma?" A surge of panic—or paranoia—spiked the hairs on his arms. Maybe he shouldn't have been so quick to let these guys in. "Are you guys talking in code or what?"

The two men exchanged stern looks again before Sean spoke. "Emma is your daughter, and she's very ill. Morgan was pregnant when she left Texas. Emma is five. We need for you to come with us."

Kyle stopped breathing. When he finally forced a breath, he stood up with weak knees and paced, his blood pressure surely off the chart. "I don't have a child." He'd been intimate with Morgan one time, and they'd both agreed it wouldn't happen again, unless they were married. "There's some sort of mistake."

"I'm sure you have a lot of questions, and we'll be happy to answer them all on the plane."

"Plane?" Kyle was still trying to process the possibility he might have a child. A sick child.

"What's wrong with the little girl?" He wasn't ready to say 'my daughter' just yet. This seemed far-fetched.

"She has a medical condition called aplastic anemia and needs bone marrow stem cells... from you, if she's going to live."

"*What?*" Kyle's knees were so shaky he had to sit back down.

Sean and Landon exchanged glances again, and Landon cleared his throat. "Other options have been exhausted. Emma's team of doctors have searched the database for an exact match, but because of her rare AB-negative blood type, a match couldn't be found. The best option is a sibling, but Emma doesn't have a brother or sister. You, as her father, would be a half match, giving her the biggest chance of beating this."

Kyle held his head in his hands as thunderclaps followed bursts of light from outside the window. His mind was formulating questions faster than he could organize the thoughts into words.

"Morgan or her parents can't help Emma. You are the one with the rare blood type who might be able to save her." Landon's eyebrows narrowed into a frown.

Kyle had always known his blood type was rare, and he gave blood as often as he could, hoping to help someone who needed it, but he couldn't have predicted this in a thousand years. "I—I... " His temples throbbed as his hands grew clammy. He'd had an anxiety attack once in his life, when he was twelve and saw a little girl on a bike get hit by a car. This felt like the same thing as his thoughts clouded into a swirl of confusion. He let go of his head and looked at Landon, then at Sean. "My bone marrow will save her life?" *A daughter? I have a child? Emma?*

"You're the best hope she's got," Landon said as he stood up.

Sean stood up also, but Kyle stayed seated, unsure if his legs would keep him upright.

"Where is she?"

Sean took a step closer to where Kyle was sitting. "We can't tell you that, Kyle, until after we are on the plane."

"What?" He finally stood up and folded his arms across his chest, but the action was mostly to calm his churning stomach. Giving himself a few moments to corral his thoughts, he said, "Two strangers show up at my door and tell me that my high school girlfriend is the mother of a child I didn't know I had. Now you expect me to travel to an undisclosed location to try to save her life." He hung his head, shaking it before he looked back at them. "How soon would I leave? I'd need to talk to my fiancée, and… " He blew out a long, windy sigh. "Oh man. Lexie. I have to tell Lexie."

"You can't, Kyle," Landon said as his eyebrows furrowed. "We need to leave right now, and you can't tell anyone."

"Uh, you're crazy. I can't just pack a suitcase and walk out the door to go wherever with you. How do I even know you're telling the truth?"

Landon and Sean stared at him with blank expressions, then they exchanged looks—again. Kyle was tired of being the third wheel in a conversation that was keeping him the dark.

"We have to leave now," Landon said as a muscle flicked in his jaw. The guy's eyes were hooded like a hawk ready to swoop down on his prey.

Kyle swallowed hard.

And I'm the prey.

Chapter Two

Lexie used her fork to dig out the chicken salad from between two pieces of bread.

"The bread is the best part of the sandwich here." Mom took a large bite of her own chicken salad sandwich. Candace White was one of those women who ate whatever she wanted and never gained weight. Lexie—regrettably—didn't inherit that gene from her mother. She had to work at staying thin.

"I know, but I'm trying to be careful between now and September. I want to be able to fit into my dress." Lexie smiled. Just the thought of being Kyle's wife kept her joyful through just about anything, even watching her mother try on sixteen dresses, not choosing any of them prior to lunch.

"I still think you kids are awfully young to be getting married, but we love Kyle." Mom shrugged. "So, I guess the heart knows what the heart wants."

"Twenty-three isn't all that young. We've already finished college and have great teaching jobs. It's time to settle down, and we both want a family."

"Plenty of time for that too," her mother said as a frown filled her face. "Have you had *the talk* with Kyle?"

Lexie knew exactly what her mother was referring to, and easing into that conversation would hamper the day much more than the rain. "No. But I will." *Please let it go, Mom.*

"You will be a great mother," her mom said quickly, as if she was having the same thought as Lexie. "But one thing at a time." She took a sip of tea, then let out an exasperated breath. "Where in the world am I going to find a dress for this wedding?"

Lexie shook her head, grinning. "I don't know, Mom. But I do know that I can't wait to be Mrs. Kyle Brossmann." She glanced at her phone on the table next to her plate, wondering why she hadn't heard from Kyle. Lexie had sent him a text over an hour ago, but as rain pelted the metal roof of the café, Lexie suspected Kyle had gone back to bed. It seemed like a day for that, and she wished she were cuddled up with him. Just holding each other, snuggling. She was proud that she and Kyle had agreed not to have sex until after they were married. It was an option that was growing less and less popular among her friends, but Lexie wanted to do right in God's eyes. She was glad Kyle shared her thoughts about the matter, even though he'd admitted to one slip up with his first girlfriend.

Morgan held a cup of water for Emma as her daughter sucked from a straw. Emma had been cleared to go home hours ago, but as was always the case, they'd been waiting around for discharge papers, instructions for home care, prescriptions, and a hoard of other information that always accompanied these unplanned hospital visits.

"Is the man coming today?" Emma leaned her head against the pillow, and Morgan nodded as she set the cup down on the tray in front of her daughter. "The man that's going to help me get well?" she added.

"Yes, he is. Remember I told you that this man has the same type of blood that you do, so that's important." Morgan and her parents had agreed not to tell Emma that Kyle was her father. It didn't seem fair to introduce Emma to a second parent, then tear her away from him again. It seemed equally as unfair to Kyle, but Morgan would do whatever it took to save Emma.

Morgan's father had gotten word an hour ago that Sean and Landon were on their way to the airport with Kyle. She couldn't even imagine what Kyle must be feeling. Would he hate her for keeping such a secret? It had been the only way to ensure that Emma would be safe. *But still.*

She wanted to be happy that Kyle had found someone to share his life with. He deserved that. Morgan was afraid to completely commit to another man since the recovery over losing Kyle had been excruciating. But she'd had Emma to focus on after she was born, which slowly eased the pain until she had stopped thinking about Kyle much at all. Until Emma turned four. It was then that her daughter's features matured in a way that reminded Morgan of Kyle. They both had big blue eyes and exceptionally long eye lashes. Emma had a perfectly proportioned nose like Kyle. Morgan was thankful for that since her nose was a tiny bit pugged. Her heart smiled when she recalled the way Kyle used to tell her what a cute nose she had. So many memories.

Emma's mouth had also taken on the same shape as Kyle's, and like his, Emma's smile lit up her face, crooking up just barely on one side, not enough that most people would even notice.

"Do Nana and Papa know the man who's coming?" Emma gazed at Morgan with curious eyes, as if this might be the most important question she'd ask today.

"No, they don't." *Forgive me, God.* Morgan despised lying, especially to her own daughter. But

Morgan loved Emma enough to protect her. How could she tell her own daughter that they had been relocated because her grandfather's life and entire family were being threatened? Her father had said that was the only way to keep everyone safe, even Kyle. Morgan hoped to spare Emma the kind of life she'd had growing up, the same way she planned to guard her heart from the type of heartache leaving Kyle had caused.

Morgan had plenty of tantrums when they'd first arrived at their new home, but they were all futile, and like it or not, this was her life. As she gazed at her beautiful daughter, she thanked God daily for this precious gift. And she begged Him daily to heal Emma.

Morgan had beat herself up for a long time for sleeping with Kyle, just once, when they were seventeen. But now, as she looked at Emma, she knew this was all just part of God's plan, and He was never wrong.

If Kyle was a match for Emma—and she prayed he was—she wondered how her father was going to handle Kyle being so close to the place they called home. Not even her grandparents knew where they were. Her father, along with Sean and Landon, had been vague about the entire plan.

Kyle stepped out of the black limousine. He was able to count on one hand the other times he'd been in such a vehicle—senior prom, a wedding, and a couple of funerals. He felt numb as the driver peeled away, leaving him with Sean and Landon. He glanced at his one piece of luggage. A girly red suitcase that Lexie must have left at his apartment. At the time, he'd grabbed the first thing he found. But now, he felt silly.

"That's the plane?" Kyle gulped as he eyed the small craft that was going to take him to wherever he was going. He'd just assumed they would be on a commercial flight.

"It's our biggest jet. Seats eight. There's a bar onboard if you need something to calm your nerves."

Kyle stood there, still trying to absorb the fact that he had a five-year-old daughter, who was terminally ill unless Kyle's bone marrow was a match for her. He wasn't a drinker, but he was sure there wasn't enough booze on that plane to calm his nerves. "Do you have a picture of her, of Emma?" The sun blazed down on them as they stood on the hot, black asphalt a few yards from the plane.

Sean shook his head, but Landon spoke up. "I do." He reached into his back pocket and took a photo out of his wallet. "Isn't she a beauty?"

Kyle had no words as he eyed the bright eyed, blonde girl in the picture. "She's beautiful," he finally said in a whisper before he offered the picture back to Landon.

"Keep it," he said, smiling.

Kyle turned his attention toward a plane that would carry him to California. "How long will I be gone?" Thankfully, he was a teacher and it was summertime. At least he didn't have his job to contend with.

"We're not sure." Sean waved to a pilot standing on the steps to the plane.

"I—I gotta call my fiancée and tell her what's going on." He'd gone this long without calling Lexie at Sean and Landon's insistence, but he couldn't get on a plane without at least telling her he was okay. "And I won't tell her where I'm going." *Not yet.* He hadn't been able to get a signal in the limo, which seemed odd. He pulled his cell phone from his pocket, but he couldn't get a call to go through.

Sean cleared his throat. "Your phone's been disabled and the service shut off."

"Say what?" The hairs on the back of Kyle's neck bristled. "Why?"

"From this point on, you can't have contact with anyone, not even Lexie. Not your mother, your grandparents, no one," Landon said.

"No deal." Kyle shook his head. "I'm not getting on a plane with two guys I don't know without telling someone what's going on."

"Those are the terms, and by being here with us, you've agreed." Sean shrugged. "We're not kidnapping you, Kyle. You can choose not to go. But if you do go, those are the rules. No contact with anyone until you return."

"What's to keep me from telling Lexie and everyone where I was when I get back?" He grunted, grinning. "Unless you're planning to just kill me after I help Emma."

Sean and Landon glanced at each other before Sean smiled. "I assure you, Kyle, no one is going to kill you."

"Well, forgive me, but you guys don't sound very convincing." Kyle folded his arms across his chest. "So… when I go missing, Lexie is going to report it. Then everyone is going to be wondering what happened to me, causing tons of grief for my family, and probably for you. Wouldn't it be better to avoid all of that and just let me call her right now?"

"Once you're on the plane, an email will be sent to Lexie from your email account, explaining to her that you need some time to think about things, about your relationship and whether or not marriage is the right step to take."

Kyle laughed. "Yeah, well, she'll never believe that. If anything, I'm the one who pushed her to get married. That's not going to fly. Our love is stronger than that, and she'll know that's not true."

"Maybe. Maybe not. But it will keep the authorities from looking for you and buy us some time." Landon nodded toward the plane. "We've got to go."

Kyle shook his head, but got in step with him on his way to the plane. "Where in California are we going?"

"LAX. Los Angeles," Sean said.

"I might need that drink after all." One thing he knew for sure... he'd find a way to contact Lexie when he got there. He was savvy enough to avoid these guys long enough to do that. So he decided to settle back and try to relax.

He was still holding the picture of Emma when the pilot started to taxi on the runway of the small, private airport. Landon and Sean were chatting with the pilot about the flight path, and just by overhearing, Kyle learned that both Landon and Sean were pilots also. That should have made him feel a little safe, but when Landon turned to pour himself a drink at the small bar to their left, Kyle saw a holstered gun.

Looking at the picture, his emotions swirled and collided, but he couldn't have lived with himself if he didn't make this trip in an effort to save Emma. *My daughter.*

Chapter Three

Morgan waited at the airport for Landon and Sean to arrive with Kyle. It was almost nine at night, but she felt at peace about Emma for now. Her daughter was home in her bed with her grandparents keeping a watchful eye on her. Morgan wondered if there would ever be a time in her life that she wasn't consumed with worry about Emma. So many times she'd tried to let go and let God, as her mother often said, but so many trips to the hospital ER kept Morgan teetering on the edge when it came to her faith. *Why can't God just make her well?*

Even though her relationship with God was on a slippery slope, she silently prayed that Kyle would be a match for Emma.

Morgan glanced at the time on her cell phone. She'd already calculated and allowed for the time changes going from Texas to California… and finally here. She wondered if Kyle knew where his final destination would be and if he'd ever been here before. As she glanced around the airport, she doubted it, unless he'd been here since she'd seen him, which was certainly possible. She suspected that Kyle's entire stay would be in the big city. She couldn't imagine her father allowing him to see where they live—on an island so private it's referred to as the 'forbidden island' by the locals.

She heaved her purse on her shoulder and looked at her cell phone again. The flight would take longer than a commercial flight, but the weather and direction of the wind could influence their arrival time by as much as an hour.

Morgan's stomach twisted in knots as she paced. She didn't think she looked much different than when Kyle last saw her, and she wondered if he'd changed. After Emma was born, it had taken a while to get rid of her baby weight, but she'd eventually lost it all and had remained about the same weight for the past four years. She fingered a strand of hair and pulled it in front of her. It was a lighter shade of blonde from all of her time in the sun, and living near a beach provided a year-round tan. There were some perks to living in a tropical paradise.

Morgan wondered what Kyle's fiancée looked like. Her father, along with Sean and Landon, knew everything there was to know about the woman—Lexie White. Morgan had the best luck getting information from Landon, but when she'd asked him about Lexie, Landon had just shrugged. "She's cute, I guess." Morgan had tried to push for more, but Landon had swerved his way out of the conversation, something Morgan suspected they taught at CIA school. Along with all kinds of other tactics that Morgan wasn't privy to.

She was surprised that her dad hadn't opted to come to the airport. Despite her father's job and ability to detach from his emotions when necessary, Neil Calhoun had loved Kyle for a long time. Morgan knew how hard this was for her. But it had to be difficult for her parents too. *So many memories.*

Kyle sat across from Landon, a small table in between them. Sean was in a nearby seat pounding away on a laptop.

"Are you going to eat that?" Landon nodded at Kyle's barely eaten sandwich and chips. He shook his head, pretty sure he'd vomit if he ate any more. He reached into his pocket and took out his bottle of pills, glad he'd remembered to grab his meds in all the commotion. Missing a dose for his heart condition wouldn't be the end of his world, but he would feel like his heart was somersaulting in his chest, more than it already was. He popped the Propranolol in his mouth.

His mind was awhirl with questions, but getting answers from Landon or Sean was like squeezing blood from a turnip. He spent a few minutes trying to organize his thoughts, then cleared his throat.

"Will Morgan be at the airport when we land in Los Angeles?" Kyle's heart fluttered at the thought of seeing her again, which made him feel a little guilty. He was in love with Lexie, and he didn't foresee Morgan changing his feelings about that. But somehow, picturing her raising their child was having a weird affect on him he couldn't identify.

Landon swiped at his mouth with a napkin, shaking his head. "No. She won't be in Los Angeles."

Kyle looked over at Sean, wondering if the older man would add anything, but he was sleeping, his head laid back against the seat and his laptop still open.

"Will she be in the vicinity when we land?" Kyle didn't try to keep the cynicism out of his voice.

"No." Landon stuffed a chip in his mouth. "But you'll see her. Eventually."

Kyle folded his arms across his chest and stared at the guy, tempted to ask Landon how old he was and how he'd landed a job with the CIA. He didn't look the part, aside from his athletic build. He had pretty-boy blond hair and not even a hint of five o'clock shadow. Nothing rough around the edges to signify he'd ever suffered more than a bad night's sleep. Kyle touched the scar on his chin, a foul ball that landed him six stitches. But even though Landon's job interested Kyle, it was far down the list.

"So ..." Kyle waited until Landon ate the last chip on the plate and met eyes with him. "Is Morgan's dad in some kind of trouble? Is that why they moved in the middle of the night? Or is he in some sort of witness protection program?" Landon stared blankly at him. "Does it really matter if I know at this point?" Kyle briefly thought about his comment he'd made earlier, joking about whether or not these two men might kill him. He couldn't imagine Morgan's father would let that happen. Neal Calhoun had been the closest thing to a father Kyle had after his own father died. But then, he wouldn't have thought the man would whisk them all away in the middle of the night, with little afterthought about how it would affect Kyle. And what about Morgan? Did it take her weeks, months…maybe a year to get over the loss? Did she think about Kyle when she was giving birth to their daughter? What about the five years that followed? His heart thumped wildly, realizing he hadn't asked a really important question.

"Is Morgan married?"

Landon shook his head. "No. She's not married."

"Boyfriend?"

Landon grinned. "No."

"I'm glad you're enjoying this. My life has been tossed upside down, and who knows where I'll end up." He thought about Lexie. His first priority would be to make contact with her somehow.

Landon stilled his expression. "Look, I know you have a lot of questions. Neal, Morgan's father, will be the one to fill you in on anything we haven't covered."

"Yeah, I know who Neal is. I've known Morgan and her parents since I was a kid."

"They're all good people." Landon glanced at Sean, who was snoring lightly, his hands still poised above the laptop keys. Then he turned back to Kyle. "Morgan is super nervous about seeing you," he said in a whisper. "If you've got any sort of anger toward her, you need to stow it before you see her. She's dealing with a tremendous amount of stress, and adding you to the mix just complicates everything even more."

Kyle wanted to bark back at him that someone needed to recognize the amount of stress he was under, but despite everything, he'd loved Morgan with all of his heart at one time, and he didn't want to cause her extra pain. He assumed that having a sick child was overwhelming. But the only thing overwhelming Kyle was fear—of losing Lexie over this.

But as much as he loved Lexie, he couldn't push a Pause button to mute thoughts about Morgan and

Emma. He wondered if he was even father material. He had no feelings for this child one way or the other, except that he could save a life, something he'd do for anyone if he were able. Emma might be his daughter, but the lack of knowledge about her made it hard for him to accept the emotional impact that he might have expected.

"I'm going to do my best not to upset her, but no promises." Kyle looked at Sean when the man shifted his weight in the seat, but once he was snoring again, he said, "If you don't want me to upset her, then maybe you need to let me tell Lexie what's really going on so I'll be a little calmer." He shrugged, raising an eyebrow. "I'm going to tell her when I get back anyway."

"You mean, if we don't kill you, right?" Landon grinned.

A shot of adrenaline backstroked through his veins until he was sure it would come out his mouth in the form of vomit.

"Kyle… everything is going to be okay. Really." Landon still spoke in a whisper. "No one is going to kill you. You have an opportunity to save your daughter's life. And you can tell Lexie all about it when you get home."

Kyle scratched his forehead. "How can that be? I haven't had contact with these people for almost six years, but it will be okay for me to tell Lexie all about them?"

"Just wait for Neal to talk to you."

"Well, I hope he clues me in better than you are." Kyle huffed, leaned his head back, and attempted to pray. But his thoughts were so jumbled, he wasn't sure God could even sort them in a way that made sense.

"Oh, there's one more thing." Landon scowled. "And we should have mentioned it earlier. Morgan is Mia. Her mother, Patricia, goes by Patty now. Neal is Alex. You'll need to get used to those names. And their last name is Smith."

Kyle stared at Landon for a few long moments. "*Mia?* Morgan doesn't look like a Mia."

"Well, that's her name now. We agreed to refer to them all by their previous names until you settled into things. But now would be a good time to associate their faces with their new names."

Kyle tried to attach the name Mia to the Morgan he'd loved. It didn't fit her. "Did she choose Mia or one of you guys?" He nodded toward Sean.

"It was selected for her."

"Wow." Kyle rolled his eyes. "Will someone be *selecting* a name for me too?"

Landon grinned. "Uh, no. You get to stay the same ol' Kyle you've always been."

I don't feel like the same ol' Kyle.

Lexie stared at the email on her phone as she trembled from head to toe. Then she re-read it for the tenth time.

Lexie,

I know this will come as a surprise, but I feel like I need some time to myself to think about things. I'm sure I'm just having a touch of cold feet, so please don't worry. We have the rest of our lives to spend together, but there are a few things that I need to take care of before we are married. Can I please ask you to just trust me about this? Our love can withstand this. Trust me, okay?

I love you,

Kyle

She'd been sitting on the couch for the past hour and jumped when there was a knock on the door. "It's open." She'd called her mother as soon as she'd received the email.

"I could barely understand you on the phone. Are you okay?" Her mother sat down beside her. Lexie showed her the email on her cell phone and waited for her to read it.

"I don't understand." Her mother handed the phone back to her, pressing her lips together for a few moments. "What does this mean?"

Lexie swiped at her swollen eyes and shrugged. "I have no idea. And I've emailed him back, sent a text message, and tried calling, but there's no answer."

"Honey, you have to have a clue. You're planning to marry this man in a few months. Did you two have a fight or something?"

Lexie wondered if she should have called Penny or one of her other friends, someone instinctively more sympathetic than her mother. "No. We didn't have a fight, and nothing has changed."

Her mother huffed, then said, "Well, you were concerned earlier today because you hadn't heard from him, not even a text. Did you have some sort of gut feeling that something was wrong?"

"Mom!" She said it louder than she meant to, enough that her mother leaned a few inches away and scowled. "Nothing was wrong. There've been plenty of times that one of us hasn't been able to text for a lot of reasons. But this…" She took her phone back from her mother and skimmed the email again. "This is bizarre." Sniffling, she tossed the phone on the couch next to her.

"Okay, okay." Mom stood up and began to pace. "Have you been to his apartment?"

"Kind of."

"What do you mean, *kind of*? It's just a few steps away. Don't you think you should go see what's up?"

Lexie stood up, straightened her crumpled pink shirt, then blew her nose. "I'm not going to snoop. And if he wanted to get away from me, he wouldn't be in his apartment right downstairs." She folded her arms across her chest and looked down. "Besides, I already went to his apartment and beat on the door, but I was too nervous to use my key."

"Chop, chop." Her mother clapped her hands twice. "Get the key."

Lexie was too desperate not to reconsider the idea, so she shuffled toward her purse on the kitchen bar. She held the key in her hand for a few moments before she said, "Okay. I'll go look. Just to make sure nothing seems off."

Her mother hurried toward the door. "I'm going with you."

A few minutes later, Lexie put the key in the lock, jiggled it, turned it back and forth, but the door didn't open. Her heart thumped against her chest as she turned to her mother, tears pouring down her face.

"The lock has been changed."

Chapter Four

Kyle stood up in the plane once it stopped. A couple more inches, and he wouldn't clear the ceiling of the jet, which Landon called a Super Midsize earlier. Both Landon and Sean had to bend over a little not to bump their heads.

He waited for the pilot to lower the steps, then Kyle followed his escorts down and glanced around. He'd never been in a private jet, so he wasn't sure of protocol, but they were a long way from the LAX main terminal. He'd noticed earlier that the pilot had taxied away from the tarmac. His mind was a thunderstorm of activity. *I need to find a way to call Lexie. I have a daughter. I'm with the CIA in a private jet. And I'm going to see Morgan after all these years.* Maybe his priorities were out of whack, but getting in touch with Lexie was at the top of his list.

"I need to go to the restroom." Kyle nodded toward the terminal as he stuffed his hands in the pockets of his jeans.

"There's a bathroom on the plane," Landon said before making his way to the pilot.

Oh yeah. They'd told him that when he boarded, but Kyle didn't leave his seat the entire flight. He turned to Sean. "Where am I staying? When will I see Morgan—I mean *Mia*?" He swallowed hard. "And the little girl."

"Soon." Sean was reading something on his cell phone and frowning.

"Okay. So, where am I staying?" He grunted. "It better be the Penthouse or Presidential suite somewhere, after all of this."

Sean stowed his phone, barely smiled, and said, "I'm sure you'll be pleased with your accommodation once we arrive at our final destination."

Kyle tried to read Sean's expression, but it was flat, and as Kyle looked around, he saw two guys refueling the plane. "Do what?" His head pounded like it might explode. He wasn't sure he could process any more information today.

Sean took a step closer to him. "Kyle, this airport isn't where Morgan and Emma are. We are just refueling."

The hairs on the back of his neck prickled. "Okay, you know what… " Kyle puffed his chest out, knowing he was no match for Sean, but wanting some answers. "You told me we were going to California!"

Sean's eyebrows bent inward as he scowled. "Lower your voice. Everything is fine."

Kyle ran through a string of curse words in his mind, but he stowed them and took a deep breath. "With all due respect, Sean…everything is not *fine*. My life just got overhauled, and now I don't even know where we're going. That's a bunch of—"

"Honolulu. That's where we are going." One side of Sean's mouth curled up. "Surely there are worse places to be going."

"I can think of worse places to be taken during a kidnapping." Kyle rolled his eyes, and under different circumstances, he'd be thrilled to be going to Hawaii.

"We told you, Kyle, no one is kidnapping you."

"Then why didn't you just tell me we were headed to Hawaii, instead of letting me believe California was our destination?"

"We wanted to be sure the situation was secure first."

Landon strolled back up to them as Kyle looked back and forth between the two men, wondering which one of them packed the most powerful punch. Just in case Kyle lost control and took a swing at one of them.

"Well, I didn't even bring swim trunks," Kyle said as he forced a fake grin.

"I doubt there will be time for swimming or walks on the beach." Landon took in a deep breath and blew it out slowly, looking at the pavement. When he looked back up at Kyle, he said, "I just pray you're a match for Emma. The doctors will do some tests, but as her parent with the same blood type, everyone is hopeful."

Kyle stared at the man. There was enough emotion in Landon's comment to know that he cared about the little girl. "Have you known Emma all of her life?"

Landon smiled as he glanced at Sean. The older man's flat expression lifted at the sound of Emma's name also. "We both have," Landon said. "She's a beautiful little person."

Kyle was quiet. He didn't know this girl. And it didn't sound like he was going to have an opportunity to get to know her. He'd do the right thing, then go back home to Lexie. But as soon as he faced the possibility that he might not see the child again, it pierced his heart. "Do either one of you have children?"

Landon shook his head, but Sean nodded. "I have two daughters and three grandchildren."

Kyle thought for a few moments. "Then, can you, for one moment, understand some of what I'm feeling? I just learned I have a daughter." He didn't think he was having the right feelings, though. Shouldn't he feel more than he was? Was he missing the paternal gene? Either way, he hoped at least one of these fellows would warm up to him a little.

"I do sympathize with your situation, Kyle." Sean nodded toward the pilot, and it looked like the refueling process was complete.

Kyle got in step with both men as they walked back to the stairs leading into the plane. "But wait… " He stopped in his tracks, forcing Sean and Landon to wait for him to finish. "After this trip, then I just leave, go back to Houston, and I never see Emma again?" Staying in his daughter's life seemed like the respectable thing to do, if it was possible. "Or, now that I'm in her life, will I be able to stay in her life? See her grow into an adult, get married?"

Landon's gaze seemed to be somewhere outside of their circle, but Sean locked eyes with Kyle. "If you are a match for Emma, the doctors will schedule the stem cell transfer. From there, you will recover, then return home. You won't see Emma again."

Kyle took a step backward, fists clenched at his side. He had no idea how he would feel about this child, but this entire charade was unfair—and just plain wrong. "How can you just calmly say that?" He was almost yelling, and maybe the events of the day had caught up with him, but he could feel tears in his eyes. "Dude, I'm on emotional overload right now. Seriously. My fiancée is at home reading some stupid email that she'll never believe." He pointed a finger at Sean. "I'd like to know exactly what that message said, by the way!" He took a breath as he put a hand to his forehead, hoping to calm the thunder. "And then I just go back home and resume my life as if none of this happened?"

Sean and Landon exchanged glances while Kyle waited for one of them to tell him to lower his voice or smack him. Landon cleared his throat.

"Yes, that's right. You'll go home with the knowledge that you have a child, but you won't ever see her again."

Are you stupid? "I'll know they are in Honolulu, and I'm sure I can find them again."

Landon folded his arms across his chest, glanced at Sean, then back at Kyle. "Morgan and Emma don't live in Honolulu. It's simply where the best hospital is located, and that's where the procedure will take place."

Kyle hung his head, shaking it.

"But…" Landon said. "We're not as cold and heartless as you think."

"I doubt that," Kyle mumbled without looking up.

"You'll have options." Sean nodded to the pilot, signifying they were ready.

"What options?"

"You can choose to stay." Sean started toward the stairs again, Landon following.

Kyle hurriedly got in step behind them. "What do you mean, *stay*? Like, Lexie and I would live in the same state as them? Or just write letters and have Emma every other weekend and holidays? What options?"

Sean lowered his head and walked into the plane. Landon turned around from where he was standing on the top step. "No, Kyle. That's not how it works. You can choose to stay with Morgan and Emma, but you could never go back to your old life. You wouldn't see your mother or Lexie again. That's the way this arrangement works. It's not really a witness protection program, but similar."

Kyle lowered his head, almost tripping on the steps. "This is crazy," he said, fighting tears. But he stayed quiet. If the little girl triggered feelings in him that he couldn't fight off, he'd figure out a way to stay in her life. Somehow. And one thing he knew for sure. He was never giving up Lexie.

Tourists paraded past Morgan in waves bigger than the morning surf. Some wore fresh leis while others still sported the cheesy fake variety. Suitcases and carry-on bags adorned with "Aloha!" stickers and "Hang Ten!" tags trailed behind hurried airport pedestrians.

Morgan brought a hand to her chest when Sean and Landon came into view on the escalator descending to baggage claim, where Morgan was standing. Seconds later, her eyes locked with Kyle's, and for a few moments, she was seventeen again, cocooned in a blanket of youthful love and absorbed by everything that went along with it. She hadn't expected this. Maybe she'd been so absorbed with Emma that she hadn't allowed herself to feel what it would be like to see Kyle after all these years. He was taller, she thought. His brown hair was shorter, and his blue eyes seemed a shade darker. But as she studied him walking toward her, she willed away any feelings lingering in her heart. He'd be gone soon enough. And this time there would be goodbyes. She glanced at Landon and Sean, but quickly refocused on Kyle. He stopped right in front of her.

"Morgan," he whispered.

"It's Mia now." She held her breath, tempted to throw her arms around him and hold on for the rest of her life. "Thank you for coming," she managed to say, her voice cracking.

"We have a daughter." Kyle said matter-of-factly, as if the realization hadn't soaked in yet.

"Emma," she said. Since her daughter was born in Hawaii, she'd always be Emma Smith. No need to change her name like the rest of them did, giving up a past without leaving a trace of the life they'd lived.

Kyle's glassy eyes couldn't mask his emotions, and Morgan wished she could tap into his mind and read his thoughts. Was there still love? Resentment? Anger?

Landon cleared his throat. "We need to get going."

Morgan didn't move or allow her eyes to drift from Kyle's, afraid that if she blinked, that he'd be gone again. He inched forward until he was close enough that Morgan could feel his breath against her skin. Cupping his hand behind her head, he drew her to him, and she clutched his shirt with both hands, squeezing her eyes closed.

"We have a daughter," he said again in a whisper.

"Yes." Morgan buried her head in his chest. "Emma."

Landon cleared his throat again, louder this time, and Morgan forced some distance between her and Kyle, then she glanced at Landon, knowing all of this was hard on him also.

Chapter Five

Lexie, a box of Kleenex, and her wedding dress sat atop her bed, and every time she thought she couldn't cry another tear, a bucketful streamed down her face. She jumped when her cell phone rang and quickly slid her finger across the Answer button on her phone. "Hello."

She waited, but there was only static. "Hello," she said louder. "Kyle?" The number wasn't his, but she stayed hopeful.

More static, then the line went dead, her small window of hope closing. She held the phone in her hand, but after thirty minutes, she finally tossed it on the bed. Everything about this situation was wrong. She'd already been to the apartment manager's office the day before, but the woman wouldn't share any information about Kyle's lock being changed, saying she couldn't discuss it with someone not on his lease. Lexie doubted that was true. It had been obvious several times in the past that the woman had a thing for Kyle. Lexie wasn't the jealous type, so it hadn't bothered her. Until now. Everything was up for grabs. *Does Kyle have someone else?* She didn't think so. *Why did his feet become suddenly cold? What does he have to take care of?*

"Please, Kyle. Call me. Please be okay," she murmured to herself.

She picked up the phone and looked at the number, then Googled 808, the area code. *Hawaii?*

It must have been a telemarketer, maybe someone trying to sell her a vacation, but she hit redial anyway, and all she heard was static.

She lay down, pulled her wedding dress toward her, and latched onto it. Then she prayed that wherever Kyle was, that he was safe.

Kyle looked out the hotel window, and if not for the mountains in the distance, he would have thought he was in Houston or any other metro city. *Couldn't they have at least sprung for a room with a view of the beach?* Sean had said this hotel was near the hospital where Emma's procedure would take place, assuming Kyle was a match.

He stared at the phone, but all his attempts to reach Lexie had resulted in one possible connection, and there'd been too much static to know if she was on the other end of the line. Anger burrowed into Kyle's heart like a tick sucking the life out of him. He was a prisoner of his own circumstances, and even though he knew Morgan—Mia—was a victim in her father's charade, he was mad at her too. She'd offered up very little information on the ride to the hotel the night before. *I deserve better than this.*

It was a selfish thought considering the situation, but as each second clicked by, his anger rose, and by the time someone knocked on the door, he was shaking with rage. He was going to tell Sean and Landon a thing or two. He yanked the door open, and his jaw dropped.

Neal was almost completely gray, and the lines of time had found their way to the corners of his eyes. "Hello, Kyle."

Taking a step backward, Kyle inched to one side so Neal could come into the room, then Kyle closed the door. He was torn between hugging the man or punching him, so he did nothing but force his jaw back into position.

"I want to see Emma." He wanted to see Morgan, too, but he didn't want Neal to read anything into that. Surely Morgan hadn't changed so much that she hadn't felt his pain the night before.

"I know this all must be such a shock to you."
Neal shook his head, frowning. "I wish that things
had gone differently, but the situation is what it is."
He smiled, but barely. "You look good, Kyle."

"I have to reach my fiancée." He pointed to the
phone. "And I know your guys disabled the phone
somehow, but Lexie is in a panic, I'm sure."

Neal scratched his forehead, and for a moment,
Kyle thought he was considering the idea, but then he
remembered how Neal always scratched his forehead
when he was thinking. "The situation isn't ideal," he
said, still rubbing two fingers parallel with the lines
above his eyebrows. "We will move things along as
quickly as possible so we can get you back home."

Kyle's hands balled into fists at his sides. "This
is all a bunch of—"

"Then why did you come?" Neal's voice rose a
fraction as he posed the question.

Kyle grunted, then shrugged. "I'm not going to
let a child die if I am able to save her, especially since
she's my…" He swallowed back a lump in his
throat."…my daughter." The word still sounded
strange, but maybe if he said it over and over again,
the action would generate more of an emotional
attachment. "When am I going to meet Emma?"

"Soon. But first we need to find out if your bone
marrow is a match. If not, we can put you on a plane
back home right away. There won't be a need for you
to meet Emma." Neal walked to the window, pushed

the curtains open more until sunlight filled the room. But even the bright island sun couldn't lift the tension from the room.

"Are you out of your mind?" Kyle walked toward Neal, but stopped when Morgan's father turned around scowling. "I just found out that I have a daughter. Do you think I'd really leave here without seeing her?"

Neal sighed. "I suppose that could be arranged."

Kyle rolled his eyes. "I would hope so." He took a step closer to Neal, realizing he didn't know this man anymore. Did he ever know him? "You were like a father to me," he said in a shaky voice.

Neal lowered his head for a few moments before he looked back at Kyle. "I can still be like a father to you while you're here."

"That isn't how parenthood works. Or so I'm told. You all stepped out of my life with no warning. Just gone!" The memories pierced his heart as he recalled walking around the Calhoun's empty house, but he forced himself to gain control and stay focused. "Does Emma know that I'm her father? Is she old enough to understand all of this?"

Neal sat down in one of two chairs on either side of a small table in the corner. A fresh orchid contrasted the sterility in the room. "She understands that she's sick, but it doesn't seem fair to tell her that you are her father, only to have you disappear from her life again."

Kyle clenched his fists at his side. "It's not like I'm being given a lot of choices."

"Life isn't fair."

Kyle slouched into the other chair. "A bit cliché, don't you think?" Arguing with Neal wasn't going to help. Kyle assumed Neal was running the show. "So, what is the plan?"

"We've pulled some strings to move this process along faster than normal, and we have a team of doctors in place. First stop is the hospital." Neal scratched his head again, frowning. "Morgan insisted that the two of you have lunch together once you get your bone marrow drawn, so I've arranged that after the hospital visit." He paused and lowered his hand. "I'll be honest, Kyle. I don't think it's a good idea for you and Morgan to spend unnecessary time together. It will make it that much harder to say goodbye. But, as you know, Morgan is strong willed, and she wasn't going to take no for an answer."

"I have no idea if she is still strong willed." Kyle gazed across the room at a picture on the wall, a woman wearing a lei and advertising a cruise to Maui. But recreation was the furthest thing from his mind. He turned to face Neal. "Why hasn't Morgan married? It seems like she'd want a father for Emma."

Neal scratched his forehead again, and Kyle was thinking it had turned into more of a tic, as opposed to part of his thinking process. "Morgan stays closed off

emotionally. She blames me for putting her in this situation."

"You can't fault her for that."

Neal frowned. "The situation isn't ideal, but keeping my family safe is always my first priority."

Maybe you shouldn't have had a child. He squashed the thought right away. *Then there'd be no Morgan. Or Emma.* "Has Morgan been serious with anyone?" It seemed unlikely to Kyle that she wouldn't have dated and gotten close to someone.

"These are questions for Morgan." Neal stood up. "I think it best that we start referring to Morgan as Mia, even in private."

Kyle nodded, although she'd always be Morgan to him.

"Let's get phase one of this operation underway." Neal straightened his back, and slowly Kyle stood up too.

"Yep. Let's get going."

Kyle needed to call Lexie. *I'll borrow a cell phone from someone.*

Morgan sat on the deck at a table for two overlooking the beach, trying to tame her hair and wishing she hadn't forgotten a hairband. A salty scent pervaded the air as foamy waves crested and broke not far from where she sat, a flock of seagulls making their presence known. She turned and caught a glimpse of her father in the distance, and a second later she saw Kyle moving in her direction, his sunglasses making it hard to read his expression. Her father walked back to his car, but Morgan was sure Landon wasn't far away.

"Everything go okay at the hospital?"

Kyle pushed the glasses up on his head and nodded to a bandage on his arm. "Yeah, I think so. And they gave me a physical. At first I thought maybe my heart medication might be a problem, but they said it wasn't."

He gazed down at her, glanced at the ocean, and finally sat down. They hadn't said a lot in the car the night before. Maybe it was because they were tired. Perhaps because they didn't know each other anymore. Their lives had gone on. Kyle's had, anyway.

"What happens if I'm not a match?" Kyle must have been balancing that thought on the tip of his tongue, Morgan thought, as the answer punched her in the gut. Again.

"We'll keep looking."

Kyle hung his head for a few moments, and when he looked up at her, he had tears in his eyes. "This is all so messed up, Morgan."

"Mia," she said in a whisper.

He gazed into her eyes, and she'd have done anything to read his thoughts. But Kyle couldn't have changed that much. She was pretty sure she knew what was on his mind.

"You're worried about Lexie, right?" Morgan reached for her glass, wishing it was something stronger than water. She wasn't a drinker, but her nerves were frayed beyond what she could have imagined.

Kyle nodded. "Yeah. I am. We're engaged, and there is no way she's going to buy that cheesy email that Landon and Sean cooked up."

Morgan smiled a little, her heart pattering in her chest as she remembered a time when Kyle felt that way about her. "Wow. You really love her."

He hung his head, then gazed out at the water. Morgan did, too, lost in memories. Hues of aqua and emerald tumbled together as the tide rolled up on pristine sand with a splash. The natural landscape was breathtaking, but today Mother Nature was only a temporary distraction.

"It's okay, Kyle. I prayed that you'd find someone, that you'd be happy. I really did."

He locked eyes with her. "I prayed about you too." His expression was flat. "Mostly that you'd contact me."

"The whole thing wasn't fair. I wouldn't speak to my father for weeks. My mother would barely talk to him either. Your mom was her best friend, and she really missed her."

"My mom missed her too."

They sat quietly for a while, the wind tossing Morgan's hair across her face, the familiar smell of saltwater swirling in the air.

"Do you think we're being punished?" A pained expression fell over Kyle's face. "I mean, for what we did. We always said we would...you know..." He raised one shoulder and slowly lowered it. "We said we would wait, until we were married."

Morgan smiled. "I used to wonder about that too." She paused as she recalled holding Emma for the first time. "Until I held Emma. I looked at her, and until that moment I had no idea that a love that strong existed. I felt closer to God at that moment than ever before in my life. I remember thinking how God loved His own son this much—or more—and sacrificed Him for all of us." She took a deep breath. "So, I can't believe that anything to do with Emma was a mistake. It was part of God's plan. But..." She wasn't sure how much to share with Kyle, but since she hadn't aired her feelings aloud, she decided to go for it. "But I don't understand God's plan. I lost you, then I was gifted with this beautiful girl, and now..." Her eyes filled with tears. "I might lose her," she said in a shaky whisper.

Kyle reached across the table and held her hand, a gesture that felt as familiar as the smell of the ocean. "We won't lose her."

Morgan noticed he used 'we', and there should have been some sort of peace in knowing that everything was coming out in the open. But as she gazed past Kyle, Morgan saw Landon far enough away that he wasn't noticeably visible, almost completely hidden behind two large plants near the entrance—yet close enough that he could be at Morgan's side within seconds. She eased her hand away from Kyle.

"Is there someone in your life Morgan?" Kyle peered across the table as he rubbed his chin.

She blinked back her earlier tears to make room for more as she looked at Landon again.

"There used to be," she said.

Chapter Six

Lexie sat next to Kyle's mother. Across a desk full of files and stacks of paperwork, a Houston police officer looked at them like they were nuts. Lexie's mother had wanted to come, too, but she had a longstanding doctor's appointment and opted to catch up with Lexie and Diana later. Lexie thought that was probably just as well. Her mother would have pounced on this cop and probably made things worse.

"I'm telling you, something isn't right. Kyle would never change the lock at his apartment without telling me, and there is no way he wrote this email." Lexie glanced at Kyle's mother and she nodded.

The cop—his badge read *Officer Scott Siewert*—leaned back in his chair, shaking his head. "Ma'am, the guy said he needs time. I'm sure he'll surface soon. We can't file a Missing Persons Report based on the information you've given me."

"He didn't write that email." She pointed to the printed copy of Kyle's email she'd placed in front of the man.

There was almost a hint of a smile. "So, someone hacked his email, changed his lock, and kidnapped him?"

"We're upset," Diana said. "We don't need sarcasm. If Lexie said Kyle didn't send that email then I believe her."

Officer Siewert stood up, and Lexie suddenly felt very small. The guy was huge, tall like a towering live oak, and as he leaned forward a little, Lexie knew their time was up. "Call me in a few days if you're still worried."

Lexie and Kyle's mother slowly stood up. Lexie supposed she'd think the same thing as the police officer if she were on the other side of the desk. But she knew, beyond a shadow of a doubt, that Kyle didn't write the email or request that his lock be changed. She'd have to keep praying he'd call her. And she'd have to keep asking God to keep Kyle safe, wherever he is.

Morgan offered a vague run-down for the past five and half years of her life, avoiding locales, and even names of people she'd known, including whomever it was that she'd been involved with for more than a year. It broke Kyle's heart to see that all the animation Morgan once had was gone, the way she used to talk with her hands, laugh out loud, and sometimes even snort when she was really tickled about something. *Robotic*. That was the word that came to mind now. He wondered how much of the change was due to her father's situation, or maybe most of it was because she had a very sick child. *Our child*.

"How'd you meet Lexie?" Morgan fidgeted with her napkin on top of the table. They'd both ordered the special—Kalua Pig. Kyle still didn't have much of an appetite, even though the offering looked a lot like pulled pork, a favorite of his.

"College," he said as he shifted his weight in the chair.

Morgan stared at him before she raised an eyebrow. "Which college?"

Kyle recalled all the dreams he'd shared with Morgan at one time, including both of them wanting to attend the same college. Kyle had held onto that. "Sam Houston State." He swallowed hard as he waited for a reaction from her, but she just bit her lip and nodded. "I'm a teacher, history."

Morgan nodded again, but didn't say anything. She'd already told him that she hadn't attended college, that at the time she was angry with her father—and pregnant. The only way she knew to rebel against her father was to refuse to further her education. Then Emma was diagnosed when she was three.

Kyle glanced around the outdoor seating area of the restaurant. "I need a restroom."

Morgan pointed over his shoulder. "I saw a sign when we came in."

He forced a smile, then headed that way. Inside the safety of this private area, he loitered around, waiting—for someone with a cell phone. There was a guy in one of the stalls, but an older man came in, and Kyle approached him.

"I'm here from Houston, and I don't have my cell phone." He nodded to the man's IPhone strapped to his belt. "I've got a bit of an emergency. Do you think maybe I could borrow your phone? I promise, two minutes tops. I need to call my girlfriend."

"Sure." The man unhooked the case and handed the phone to Kyle. He typed in Lexie's number as fast as he could, but hit End when the door to one of the stalls creaked open and closed.

Kyle lowered his gaze and handed the stranger his phone. "Thanks, but never mind." He stuffed his hands in the pockets of his jeans and turned to Landon, who was glaring at him.

After the older guy left, Landon said, "Maybe once you meet Emma, you won't feel the need to put everyone's life in danger."

Kyle could feel the burn in his cheeks. "I don't want to put anyone's life in danger. I want to let Lexie know that I'm okay, and I'm going to keep trying until I succeed."

Landon took a step closer, a muscle tensing in his jaw, along with a large enough stride to send Kyle a step backward. "It's my job to protect this family, specifically Mia and Emma."

"Can't I just call her and tell her I'm okay? I don't even have to tell her where I'm at."

Landon's expression was one of pained tolerance as he squinted his blue eyes. "You just told a complete stranger that you're from Houston."

Kyle sighed, feeling stupid. "Whatever." He turned and left the restroom, deciding to think on this, not wanting to put anyone in harm's way, but talking to Lexie was a need, not a want. He slid into his chair, slouching into the cushioned back, and eyed his Kalua Pig. Morgan hadn't touched hers yet.

"I ran into our chaperon in the bathroom," Kyle said as he picked up his fork. "Or babysitter. Whatever you want to call him." He opened his mouth to take a bite but felt the daggers Morgan was throwing his way, her brown eyes narrowing into tiny slits. "What?" He put the fork down and gazed across the table.

"That *babysitter* has kept me and Emma safe for five years. He's also been a huge comfort to me during all of this. He'd protect me and Emma with his life, and not because it's his job, but because he cares about us." She gazed out at the crashing waves as she fingered a locket around her neck.

Kyle wondered whose picture she wore around her neck. *Probably Emma's.* He lowered his head, shook it, then looked back up. "I'm sorry. I'm glad that he looks after you and Emma. I'm just worried about Lexie, and it irritates me that I can't make one simple phone call to her." He rubbed his chin, his mind swirling about ways to make that happen. Landon couldn't be with him every second of every day. He didn't think.

"I'll talk to Landon and see if there's any way someone can get word to her, without sacrificing Emma's safety."

Kyle stared at her, still waiting for some profound feeling to overtake him and catapult him into the world of fatherhood, a place where he'd put his life on the line for Emma. *Isn't that what I'm doing, though?*

He leaned his head back until he was staring into a cloudless, blue sky. Sighing, he readjusted his gaze to Morgan, really took in her features. He should have been thrilled that she was going to go to bat for him about Lexie. But right then, at that moment, the way the wind tossed her blonde hair, the way she was looking at him, memories flooded his mind. "We had so many dreams," he said in a whisper, a voice that seemed to trail into the air and out to the ocean.

She smiled. "Yes, we did."

They were quiet for a while. Kyle finally took a bite of his pork. It tasted a little like pulled pork back home, but with a smokier flavor. Morgan wrapped a small amount around her fork and finally took a bite also.

"Pretty bracelet," Kyle said, not usually one for small talk, but it was a cool bracelet. He could feel them both taking silent trips backward, and it wasn't going to do any good to rehash the what-ifs.

Morgan glanced at her wrist. "Thanks."

Kyle took a closer look. "Are those all shells?" They were beautiful, but he'd never seen anything quite like them. Bright pink shells no bigger than the eraser on a pencil were interspersed with pink and white striped shells about the same size.

Morgan held her wrist up, twisting it so he could see it from all angles. "Yeah, all shells. My mom made it from shells she's collected where we live." Her eyes rounded for a few seconds as she pressed her lips together. Then she blinked and cleared her throat.

Kyle wondered if she was going to admit her mistake, that she'd given him a clue. He eyed the bracelet again. There were only two types of shells on Morgan's wrist. They had to all come from the same place.

"It's okay," he said. "You didn't spill the beans, so don't add that to your list of things to worry about."

She gathered her hair at the nape of her neck and slung it over her shoulders, but several strands took flight and swept across her face anyway. "It's hard to keep anything from you."

Well, you've done a pretty good job of it. Kyle finished chewing and swallowed. "Did your dad *do* something? I mean, what could possibly lead to all this secrecy?"

"I don't know." There was no hesitation in her response. Kyle believed her right away. She set her fork down on her plate when her phone rang in her purse.

Kyle finally took another large bite as Morgan rummaged for her phone. Once she'd answered, the call lasted less than a minute.

"You're a match," she said after she hit End. Then she covered her eyes with one hand as she stretched her other hand out to Kyle. He grabbed her hand and held it tightly as her lip trembled. When she uncovered her eyes, she dabbed at the tears pooling in the corners, letting go of his hand. "You're going to be the one to save our daughter."

Maybe it was the way she said it, or the fact that she was crying. Maybe it was relief mixed with fear, spurning some unidentifiable emotion that was foreign to Kyle. He didn't think he told his legs to move, but the next thing he knew, he'd rounded the table, she'd stood up, and Kyle pulled her into his arms. "Yes, I'm going to save our daughter."

For the first time since he'd learned he had a child, Kyle allowed himself to feel the meaning in that statement. And for the first time since he'd arrived, he decided he was going to make Emma the priority. Everything would be back to normal when he went home. Lexie would understand, and Emma would be well. But as Kyle held Morgan in this surreal world he'd entered, he was sure nothing would be normal again.

Lexie stood beside the guy she'd hired to break into Kyle's apartment, knowing the snippy apartment manager wouldn't waste any time having them both thrown in jail if they were caught. Lexie had taken a chance and asked the young groundskeeper if he wanted to make some quick cash.

"Can you go any faster?" she said in a whisper in the partially lit hallway outside the apartment. She hadn't told her mother or Kyle's mother that she was going to become a criminal if that's what it took to find out what happed to Kyle. Diana had said earlier that she was researching private investigators, but Kyle's mother didn't have the kind of money to actually hire one, nor did Lexie. If things became more desperate, Lexie might ask her parents for help.

She was a little surprised that her mother hadn't offered to do more, but Lexie's parents weren't fond of giving up money.

"You're in." The young guy pushed the door open, then ran his hand through long strands of dark hair.

Lexie handed him a hundred dollars, cringing that she was encouraging this teenager to break the law. But he'd barely taken the money when Lexie scooted past him and into Kyle's apartment. She closed the door quietly behind her, then hit the lights, expecting to see toppled furniture, a smashed lamp, maybe the bookcase overturned. But as she scanned the living room, nothing looked out of order, and even the remote control for the television was in its designated spot on the coffee table. *Kyle, where are you?*

She scurried from room to room with no idea what she was looking for. After about ten minutes of aimless searching, she flung herself onto the couch. Guilt nipped at her.Even though this was to be her home in a few months, it seemed like a huge invasion, barging into Kyle's apartment this way. She leaned her head back against the couch and prayed.

I need help, God. What should I do? Is Kyle in danger? Am I misreading everything? Does he really want time away from me or have cold feet? Please, Lord, give me the eyes to see things clearly, the ears to hear Your wisdom, and the courage to remain strong and faithful amidst any challenges I might face.

After a while, she shuffled around Kyle's apartment, got a drink of water, and decided this was a waste of time. She'd sunk to a new low, but surely Kyle would understand. Once she found him. Her stomach rolled and tumbled as she walked toward the front door, an uneasy swirling that terrified her. *If anything happened to Kyle...*

She pulled the front door open, but turned for one last look around. Something shiny underneath the coffee table caught her eye, a shiny silver object about the size of a dime. Closing the door, she made her way to the table, reached down and picked up a cufflink. Turning it over and over in her hand, she didn't think Kyle owned any cufflinks, and it seemed odd for one to be in the living room. There was something written on the back, but it was way too small for her to see.

Lexie fumbled around in her purse until she found her cell phone. She set the cufflink on the coffee table and took a picture. Her hand trembled as she enlarged the photo on her phone. And as she read the inscription, her pulse picked up. Kyle had never been to Niihau Island, that Lexie knew of. She Googled the island and found out where it was. Alarms sounded loudly in her head. It was an island in Hawaii. And Lexie had gotten a phone call from a Hawaii area code. *Coincidence?* She didn't think so.

Chapter Seven

Kyle's feet were rooted to the tile floor outside of Emma's hospital room. She—his daughter—was only there for more testing, now that they'd learned Kyle was a match. Morgan had met him in the parking lot, and Landon agreed to give them some time alone together while he parked.

"She's just here for the day, but there's a lot of waiting around and they had a vacant room." Morgan shrugged. "It's more comfortable in here." She reached for the door handle, and Kyle grabbed her arm.

"Wait." His heart thumped wildly in his chest. "I know she doesn't know who I am. But does she know…?" Sweat pooled across his forehead as the relevance of the next few minutes slammed into him like a Mac truck.

"She knows you're the man who will make her feel better." Morgan eased out of his grip, then put her hand on his arm. "Kyle, it will be fine. And remember to call me Mia, even in front of Emma—especially in front of Emma. She's never known me as anyone else."

Kyle took a deep breath and followed Morgan into the room, his eyes instantly locking with the little girl sitting on the bed. She was wearing a pair of white shorts with a pink blouse. Her feet hung over the side of the bed, her toes curled into a pair of pink flip-flops. Golden ringlets of hair were pulled into short pigtails on either side of a pale face offset by bright blue eyes. Morgan had already told him Emma had endured a round of chemo in preparation for a transplant, and that Emma's hair was still growing in, thinner than before. Ultimately, the transplant hadn't occurred due to medical reasons Kyle didn't completely understand. He hoped there wouldn't be a problem this time. It just seemed wrong that any child should have to go through chemotherapy.

She was a cute kid, and Kyle didn't think he felt that way just because she shared his genes. But there was no doubt that Emma was sick. Morgan had explained the symptoms of asplastic anemia. Emma had bruises on her tiny pallid arms and legs, very little color in her face, and she was frail.

"Emma, this is the man we've told you about, Mr. Brossmann." Morgan went to her daughter and placed the back of her hand against Emma's forehead, but only for a couple of seconds.

Kyle forced his eyes away from Emma's and looked at Morgan. "Does she have to call me Mr. Brossmann? Maybe just Kyle?" Dad wasn't an option, and Kyle felt relieved about that at the moment. Anything else added to his overloaded heart and mind could cause him to unravel completely.

"Sure." Morgan smiled, then folded her hands in front of her. Kyle held her gaze for a surreal few moments.

"Mr. Kyle, thank you for coming a long way from your home to help me to get well." Emma barely smiled, but when she did, Kyle's insides swirled and flipped. Her tiny voice was as dainty as she was. He had a strong urge to hug her, but he had no idea what was appropriate.

"You're welcome." He forced a smile as he glanced at Morgan. "Um, how do you feel?" Kyle faced off with twenty-five seventh graders for a good part of the year, and he'd been told he was good with children. But he'd never felt so out of sorts as he did right now.

"I'm hungry."

Morgan let out a small gasp as she lifted up on her toes. "That's great, Sweetie. What do you want? I'll get you whatever you want."

Kyle took a deep breath and made his way to a chair. He'd never been so wobbly on his feet, until the past couple of days. He remembered his father watching reruns of a TV show called The Twilight Zone when he was a kid. Weird shows with people in unusual situations. Kyle felt like a participant in his own episode. *Morgan is a mom.* He'd barely had the thought when his stomach flipped again. *And I am a dad.*

"Chocolate ice cream," Emma said. And when her face lit up in a smile, Kyle was glad he was sitting down. An odd feeling settled over him in a way that seemed like it should feel good. Something warm cocooned around his heart, holding it, yet melting it at the same time. Before he liquidized into a puddle on the floor, he forced a burst of adrenaline to cool his heart. *Self preservation.* He didn't want to get close to Emma.

But as Kyle stared at this child of his, he wasn't sure that would be an option.

Morgan knew better than to leave Emma alone with Kyle. They'd all told Emma how important it was not to tell anyone where they lived, especially the man who was coming to help her. But that was a lot of pressure for a little girl, even one who is healthy and well. And Morgan had already slipped up at lunch, so she knew how easy it was to do.

They all turned when the door to Emma's room opened, followed by heavy footsteps. Emma jumped from the bed and ran to Landon. It was the fastest Morgan had seen her move in the past couple of weeks.

"Landon!" Her voice had a signature squeak normally, but even more so when she was around her 'bodyguard' as she called him.

"Hey, Emmie Lou." Landon scooped Emma into his arms and kissed her on the cheek. Morgan turned to Kyle.

"Her middle name is Louise, and Landon has called her Emmie Lou since she was born." Her eyes drifted back to Landon, then over to Kyle, then back to Landon, as her past collided with what had nearly been her future. Emma loved Landon, as much as Morgan did, maybe more. The breakup had been hard on everyone. But as she refocused on Kyle, there was still pain where he was concerned, even all these years later. She'd vowed to never get that close to anyone again. But having him here was stirring feelings she hadn't expected. What-ifs were all over the place. Her father would give Kyle an opportunity to stay, to be a father to Emma. Morgan wondered if he would even consider the offer. It was a horrible position to be put in; leave your fiancée forever or never see your daughter again. And what about Morgan and Kyle? Was there a chance they'd fall in love again? Could she open her heart again to her first true love? She slowly looked at Landon, and as their eyes locked, she could see the same questions in his gaze.

"Let's go get our girl some ice cream," Landon said, and Morgan instinctively started to go with them, but stopped.

"Um. Are you going to be okay for a few minutes? If a nurse comes in, can you let her know we went to get ice cream?"

Kyle nodded.

"Do you want some?"

"Nah. Ya'll go ahead."

Kyle didn't move for a full minute after the trio left. He stared at the phone, and he'd never wanted or needed Lexie more than right now, but he couldn't help but wonder if this was some sort of test. Landon had made sure he was in the bathroom earlier when Kyle tried to borrow a phone. And now, they just leave him alone with a phone three feet away?

He stood up and paced, then finally picked up the phone and listened to the dial tone. *It works.* Slowly he pressed Off and set the phone back on the table next to the bed, then walked to the window. As he gazed past the buildings that partly obstructed his view of the ocean, he thought about how he'd always wanted to visit Hawaii. *Here I am, and I just want to go home.*

He leaned his head back, stared up at the ceiling, and blew out a long breath before he refocused on the phone again. The temptation to call Lexie was almost too much to resist, but he couldn't bear the thought of putting Emma, Morgan, or any of them in danger.

It hadn't taken much for Kyle to figure out that Landon was the person Morgan had been involved with. In the few minutes Landon had been in the room with them, he noticed the looks going back and forth between them. It angered him that Landon had hurt Morgan, but there was also some sort of twisted relief that Morgan hadn't given her heart completely to someone else, which made no sense since Kyle was madly in love with Lexie.

Morgan sat down in the waiting room next to Landon, who was finishing his second ice cream cone, while Emma made her way to the toys in the far corner.

"I don't think you should be testing Kyle this way." She spoke in a whisper so Emma wouldn't hear, thankful they were the only ones in the room. "I'm sure he's calling his girlfriend. And if he's not calling from the phone in Emma's room, there are plenty of other phones in the hospital."

"We just want to know if he's going to put Emma's safety and needs first." Landon's gaze bordered on a glare before he shoved the last of the cone in his mouth.

"It doesn't really matter if he does or doesn't. Either way, he's agreed to this procedure. Then he'll go back home to Lexie, and that's that." She shrugged as she tried to keep her expression level and void of all the emotion she'd bottled up over the past two days.

"Will he? Go home?" Landon paused, his eyes now fixed on Emma. "Or will Emma steal his heart too?" He turned to Morgan, the muscles in his neck tensing at the base of his square jaw. "Or maybe the two of you can make a go of it."

Morgan wanted to tell Landon that she was having those same thoughts, but why twist the knife in Landon's open wound any more than she had? "That's not going to happen."

Landon turned to her as the professional mask he usually wore slowly retracted, revealing the tenderness of the man she loved. "I want you to be happy, Mia. I love you and Emma, you know that. But I'll step aside and request a transfer somewhere else, if you can have a life with Kyle, the three of you as a family."

"No." Just the thought of Landon leaving set her insides on fire. "No," she repeated, shaking her head. She'd broken up with Landon three months ago, following two years of an infatuation between them that escalated into something much more. At first, she'd thought her feelings for Landon came about because of the way he loved Emma, the way he protected both of them. But then she'd realized she was in love with the man, not the bodyguard or CIA agent. Just Landon. It was then that she began to pull away. Her heart wasn't up for grabs again. But Kyle being here was stirring up emotions she hadn't expected. She wasn't sure if it was the bond of having a child together, the fact that he was marrying someone else, or pure jealousy that his life had gone on just fine without her, and she couldn't commit to the man she loved.

Until now, she hadn't made time to psychoanalyze her situation. Did she avoid committing to Landon out of fear of losing him? Were there unresolved feelings about Kyle? Lost in thought, she jumped when Kyle entered the waiting room. He slowed his steps as he walked by Emma, who barely noticed him.

"A nurse came by while ya'll were gone." Kyle's eyes shot to Emma again before he took a few more steps toward Morgan and Landon. "But it was actually me she came to see. I'm going to have to get some shots that will build up my stems cells prior to the transplant."

Kyle sat down on the other side of Morgan and propped his elbows on his knees before he lowered his forehead to his hands. He had to be exhausted, physically and mentally. Morgan wished she could hold his hand. She wished she could hold Landon's hand too. Both were men she loved in confused capacities, remnants of her past fused with the present, leaving her uncertain about her future.

Morgan glanced at Emma before she looked back at Kyle. He took a pill bottle from his pocket and popped the blue and white pill in his mouth. Another reminder of their past and the many messages she'd left for him. She smiled a little. He still didn't need any water to wash it down.

"I didn't call Lexie," Kyle said without lifting his head. "Just in case that was some sort of test or something."

Morgan glared at Landon, but he wouldn't look at her. He was watching Emma quietly building a tower of blocks that looked like it might topple over any second. She elbowed him until he turned her way, then mouthed. "Help him."

Landon sighed. Then shook his head.

Morgan loved this man, but she wondered if she'd ever get past the power of the position he held, where sometimes things just weren't negotiable. She reached into her purse, pulled out her cell phone, then elbowed Kyle this time.

He straightened in the chair as she pushed the phone toward him.

"Call Lexie."

"What?" Kyle scowled as his eyes shifted to Landon. He didn't reach for the phone, and Landon also had a sour look on his face.

Morgan stood up, tossed her phone in the seat so hard that it fell and hit the carpeted floor. "I need peace. I need Kyle to stay focused, and he deserves a chance to get to know Emma." She lowered her voice to barely above a whisper. "And not while he's stressing about his own situation at home and missing his fiancée."

"Fix this, Landon. Do something."

She hurried to Emma about the same time all the blocks fell over, scooped her into her arms, and left the two men in the waiting room, both with dropped jaws.

Chapter Eight

Landon stood up right away and took two or three steps toward the door, but then stopped and turned around. Kyle eyed the phone on the floor, unsure whether to pick it up.

"Don't call your fiancée from that phone." Sighing, Landon scratched his forehead. "I'll talk to Sean and see about getting you a secure line."

Kyle stood up and walked toward him. "I see on the news all the time that terrorists communicate in code, so I don't understand why I can't call Lexie."

"You don't understand a lot of things." Landon stood taller, if that was possible, then headed toward the door.

"Hey." Kyle caught up to Landon just as he reached for the door handle. "I could do without the attitude." He took a deep breath and released it slowly. "Is contacting Lexie really going to put Emma and Morgan in danger?"

Landon scowled. "Mia. Her name is Mia. And you can probably make a phone call to Lexie on a secure line. But the call isn't the issue. Lexie is the issue. Every contact with the outside world puts Mia and her family in danger. I don't know how much Alex told you, but I can tell you this... Alex was undercover for a long time, and some really bad people found out, the type of people who aren't going to give up looking for him. Ever."

It took Kyle a few seconds to make the connection that Alex was Neal, Morgan's father. "Lexie would never do anything to put anyone in danger. And I trust her completely. I know everything about her. She's going to be my wife."

One corner of Landon's mouth curled up. "I doubt you know everything about her."

Kyle grit his teeth as the veins in his neck tensed. "There is nothing worse than a person in a position of power who uses it to torment others. I know everything I need to know about Lexie."

Landon's expression went flat, void of emotion, something he was able to do within a half second. "Is that what you think I'm doing, tormenting you?" He stepped closer to Kyle, his chest puffed out as his face turned red. "I don't care what you think. The only reason you're here is for Emma." He paused. "Right?"

Now it was Kyle whose mouth took on a saucy grin. "You're afraid I'll choose to stay, and even though you broke up with Morgan, you don't want me in her life. You don't want her, but you don't want anyone else to have her."

Landon held out his arm like he was going to grab Kyle around the neck, but he pulled back and held both arms rigid at his sides. "I didn't break up with *Mia*. She broke up with me. I love her, and I love Emma like she's my daughter."

Kyle held his position, but when Landon blinked his eyes a few times, Kyle thought he might actually cry. The big, tough CIA man was getting watery. "Then why does Mor—*Mia* get so upset when she talks about how she was involved with someone? It was pretty easy to see that it was you by just watching the way you two look at each other." He shrugged. "I just assumed you were the one who broke up with her."

"Well, you assumed wrong." Landon gained his composure quickly. "Mia's closed off her heart. She says she's afraid of getting hurt. But I'm wondering if that's the gist of it, or if it has something to do with you."

Landon's comment made Kyle's heart sing a little, then Lexie's gorgeous face flashed in his mind's eyes and a wave of guilt washed over him.

"I'm not staying. I'm going back to Lexie. I'm sure that *Mia* is afraid of getting hurt again, but I'm not the one who hurt her. It's not like I broke up with her and fled. If someone is at fault, it's her father."

Landon let out a long burst of air he'd seemed to be holding. "I'll go find you a secure line."

Kyle put a hand on the door, closing it before Landon could pull it all the way open. "No. I'm not going to call Lexie." He heard the words slip from his mouth, and he wanted to take them back, but a driving force wouldn't allow it. "I'm not going to be the one to put Emma, or any of them, in danger." Something niggled him. "Is there something I need to know about Lexie?"

Landon rubbed his chin as he shifted his weight and avoided Kyle's eyes. "No," he said before he forced the door open and left.

Kyle didn't move, unsure whether or not to believe the guy.

Lexie sat on her parents' couch, all of them quiet. Even her outspoken mother seemed at a loss for words. Finally, her father spoke up.

"Sweetheart, it could all be coincidental. The phone call from Hawaii and the cufflink with Niihau Island engraved on it. If Kyle hasn't been to Hawaii, then the cufflinks could be a gift from someone. And the phone call could have been a telemarketer. You know we all love Kyle, and his leaving is a reckless thing to do, but I think you have to accept the fact that the boy's got cold feet and he's off somewhere sorting things out in his mind."

Lexie didn't even realize she was shaking her head, until it started to pound again, the way it had for the past week. She'd called the unhelpful police officer again, but he remained—unhelpful. "I know Kyle, and I trust our love. He doesn't have cold feet."

Lexie's mother tucked her feet underneath her on the other end of the couch and cleared her throat. "Honey, I'm going to have to agree with your father. What does Kyle's mother think? I'm sure she's worried sick, but what are her thoughts about all of this?"

"Of course, she's worried." Lexie tried to keep the snappiness from her voice, but when her father grimaced, she knew she hadn't been successful. "She has a wealthy cousin that she hasn't spoken to in years, but when she contacted him, he offered to chip in for a private investigator to look for Kyle." *Hint, hint.* "Apparently he isn't as wealthy as Diana thought, or he's fallen on hard times. Either way, she's still short on the retainer to hire help."

"Did you know that Niihau Island is referred to as the forbidden island? There's not even two hundred people living there, and it's mostly closed off to anyone except for residents' relatives and invited guests." He paused. "I Googled it."

Nice way to change the subject, Dad. "I know. I looked it up on the Internet too."

They all grew quiet again. Lexie heard the Cuckoo clock in her old bedroom crow six times. Her stomach rumbled and growled, but she hadn't been able to eat much.

"Maybe this is for the best," her mother said, followed by a heavy sigh.

Lexie put a hand on her chest as she fought to swallow back tears. "How can you say that?"

Her mother twisted on the couch to face Lexie. "Honey, we love Kyle. You know that. Originally, I thought you two needed to wait a while longer to get married, but I can see how much you love each other. But Lexie, you've never been completely honest with that boy."

Lexie's heart missed a beat. Then another beat. Then it felt like it stopped and she was dying. "How can you even bring that up right now?"

"Starting a marriage while keeping a secret that big just isn't healthy." Her father forced the footrest of his recliner to the floor, then sat taller and leaned forward. "You need to tell him, Lexie. He's going to find out."

"I know," she said in barely a whisper. "And if I can find him, I will." She should have done so a long time ago, but there'd never seemed to be a good time. Fear had wrapped around her like a boa squeezing the life out of her every time she'd tried to tell Kyle her one secret, the only thing she'd ever kept from him. But right now, she just prayed he was safe.

Morgan's mother hugged Kyle so tight that he couldn't breathe.

"It is so good to see you." Patricia—*Patty*—cupped his cheeks in her hands, smiling. He'd always called her Mrs. Calhoun anyway. *Smith,* he reminded himself. "You're as handsome as ever," she said. Patty backed away and sat down in a chair across from Kyle's hospital bed, where he'd spent the past four days. "I'm so sorry that you've been alone these past few days. Emma has been sick to her stomach. She gets really down and out sometimes because her immune system is weak. It was taking both Mia and me both to take care of her." She grimaced a little. "This wasn't the best time for *Alex*..." She waited, as if to make sure Kyle knew Alex was Neal."... and Sean to get called out of town, but they'll be back before the transplant. How are you feeling? I understand they kept you in the hospital because you were having some side effects from the medication they're giving you."

He nodded. "Yeah. Mostly headaches and nausea. But I don't really think I need to be in the hospital. Is Emma okay now?" He was worried about the girl. Maybe his paternal gene was kicking in after all.

"She's doing much better." Patty smiled as her eyes filled with tears. "Kyle, the circumstances surrounding the way we left so quickly must have been devastating for you. It was for all of us, also, and I know you were left with a lot questions." She blinked her eyes, forcing the tears back. "How is your mom doing? Alex has kept an eye on all of you, so I know she never remarried. But is she okay?"

Kyle wasn't sure whether to be grateful or creeped out. "Yeah, she's okay. She missed you for a long time."

Patty lowered her gaze. "I still miss her," she said softly before she looked back up at Kyle. "And I know there is a part of Mia that will always love you. You must be so confused and upset about all of this."

"It's not ideal," he said as his stomach roiled and churned. "I think I'm going to be sick." He hurried out of bed and toward the bathroom, hoping his hospital gown was covering his backside. But flashing Patty was the least of his worries as his stomach rejected the lunch he'd eaten earlier. He threw up. Over and over again.

"Can I get you anything, Kyle?" Patty talked to him through the closed bathroom door.

"No." He hurled again and reminded himself that he had a daughter who was very sick. This was nothing compared to that. Another round of heaving, and he finally washed his face and exited the bathroom. Patty was standing by the bed with a hand over her mouth.

"They said this might happen," she said. "Some people have some fairly strong side effects from the medications they use to pump up your stem cells."

Kyle shuffled in his socked feet back to the bed and sat down. "It's okay." He allowed himself a long look at Patty. She looked exactly the same, as if Kyle had been at their house the day before, back in Houston. "I guess Mor…uh, Mia…is at home taking care of Emma?"

"Yes. She wanted to come instead of me, but when Emma feels that bad, she wants her mommy." Patty smiled. "And I wanted to see you anyway." Pausing, she smiled a little. "I hear you're getting married."

Kyle nodded. "Yeah, her name is Lexie." He was sure Patty already knew that. "We're planning to get married in the fall."

Patty nodded, but Kyle could see the sadness in her eyes.

"I guess I'd always thought you'd end up being my mother-in-law some day."

"Me too," she said barely above a whisper without looking at him.

They were quiet for a while. Finally Kyle asked, "Why do you think Mia broke up with Landon?"

Patty stiffened from the chair she'd sat down in. "Mia told you about Landon?"

"No. Not really. She told me she'd had someone in her life, but not anymore. Landon sort of spilled the beans about that, but I was already onto both of them. "It's the way they look at each other." Lexie flashed into his mind again.

Patty smiled. "Landon is a wonderful man. But I think that there is a fine line between protection and control, and sometimes Mia doesn't want to be controlled."

Despite everything, Kyle chuckled. "That doesn't surprise me."

"But…" Patty locked eyes with Kyle. "I'm not sure she ever got over losing you. I know she's closed her heart somewhat, or that's what she says, that she doesn't want to get close to anyone after what happened with you. But Landon would never be yanked out of her life. If anything, in that regard, he is the perfect person for her. That's why I think that you still hold her heart, or at least a part of it, and maybe she isn't being completely truthful with herself."

Kyle didn't know how to respond. His emotions were all over the place. "Maybe because we were each other's first love." He knew he still had feelings for Morgan, and he always would. But when he tried to envision a life without Lexie, he just couldn't do it.

"Maybe," Patty said, then a nurse walked in.

"How's our boy?" Nurse Karen was about Patty's age, and Kyle already knew that she had four boys; six, nine, twelve, and fourteen. She'd been the only person Kyle had really talked to. Landon had been in and out, and Kyle knew he was hovering around all the time. Except today. He hadn't seen him in a while. But otherwise, it was just the two nurses rotating shifts. Francine, the other nurse, wasn't particularly friendly.

"I've been throwing up a lot." Kyle opened his mouth when the thermometer grew near. He'd learned the drill. Next was blood pressure.

"I'll be here in Honolulu for a while, so I'll come check on you later." Patty stood up, then kissed him on the forehead before she left.

Again, Kyle felt like he'd just been at Patty's house, eating dinner with the family, Morgan and him holding hands under the table. *So familiar.* He closed his eyes and pictured a life with Morgan, pushing Lexie as far from his mind as she was geographically. But while he waited to see whose image would rise to the forefront, the face that strolled into his mind easily was Emma's.

Chapter Nine

Two days later and with full island sun, Morgan walked along the beach with Kyle. His body had finally recharged itself after the side effects of the meds. She wanted to hold his hand, if for no other reason than to signify their combined efforts to get Emma well.

Glancing over her shoulder, she spotted Landon and Emma downwind of them. Emma busied herself pointing at shells and critters at the edge of the water, and it warmed Morgan's heart to see her daughter feeling so much better. Emma and her bodyguard were far enough away to give Morgan and Kyle some privacy, but close enough that Landon would see Morgan holding Kyle's hands, if they did. She'd never do anything to hurt Landon, but her memories continued to collide with what the future might hold. They were quiet as they met almost head on with a group of tourists, maneuvering closer to the water so they didn't run into them. Morgan regretted that Kyle wouldn't be seeing more of the islands while he was here. *Or will he?*

"I'm sorry you were left by yourself for a few days." She pulled a strand of hair from across her face, reached for a twisty on her arm, then wrangled the whole mess into a ponytail.

"Uh, you wouldn't have wanted to be around me anyway. I was busy throwing up a lot." Kyle turned to her. "But your mom stayed with me most of the day, so." He paused, shrugging. "It was nice to be mothered since my own mom can't be here. And it reminded me of that time I fell off of my skateboard right in front of your house when we were kids. Your mom is the one who doctored me up."

"I remember that day." Morgan gazed out over the ocean as the waves lapped at her bare feet. "I remember lots of things."

"Are we going to play the 'what if' game?"

Morgan forced a smile. Two large parts of her heart were trailing behind her, but a third was walking beside her. "I guess we could, but everything that's happened up to now has led us to this moment. I'm so angry with God and so grateful to Him too." She glanced over her shoulder. "This will be the last walk on the beach Emma will have for a long time. She'll be in the hospital for at least a month after the transplant."

Kyle looked over his shoulder for a long while. "If all goes as planned, she'll go on to live a full life, a healthy life?"

"If all goes as planned," Morgan said, smiling, as she studied Kyle's expression. "She's beautiful, isn't she?"

He nodded, then finally faced forward again. "I know you can't tell me, but you must be staying close by. Can I at least ask if this is your first time to Hawaii too?"

Morgan swallowed hard and chose her words carefully. "We've been here for a while anticipating your arrival." She'd basically avoided the question. She tried not to lie when she was questioned, but instead to offer a variation of the truth. "But I've seen some of the other islands since we've been here. You'd like Maui and the other islands better than this one." She nodded to the tall buildings to their right. "But we needed to be at the best facility for the transplant, and that's here in Honolulu."

They walked quietly for a while. She'd always thought she knew Kyle so well, but time had a way of altering everything, and right now, she had no idea what he was thinking about. Lexie, most likely. Morgan wanted to feel sympathy for the woman Kyle was going to marry. But a tinge of jealousy nipped at her also.

"So…" Kyle stopped, leaned over, and rolled his jeans up a little. When he stood up, he locked eyes with her. "When this is all over, I just get on a plane to go home. I won't ever see you or Emma again. And I'm supposed to do this because it's the right thing to do. I'll tuck my feelings away…" He took a deep breath."…and walk away from you and Emma. Again."

Morgan's heart fluttered as she tried to read into his statement. Was he going to miss them both? With little regard for anyone else, she blurted out the first thing that came to mind. "Then just stay."

They stood facing each other, the ocean swirling around their ankles, and the briny smell of the ocean wafting up their nostrils. And it took everything in Morgan's power not to kiss Kyle in the most inappropriate way. He was in love with someone else, and Landon wasn't far away—but at the moment, the only thing that kept her from doing so was her daughter. She looked over her shoulder at Emma skipping along beside Landon. Her daughter wouldn't understand. And Landon surely wouldn't either.

"I'm considering it."

Morgan's mouth fell open. "You're considering staying?" Surely, she'd misunderstood.

Kyle's eyes cut past her to Landon and Emma before he refocused on Morgan." Why can't Lexie and I live wherever you live—or wherever you and

Landon live—however that plays out, then we can all be a part of raising Emma?"

Morgan's heart dropped to the pit of her stomach. She'd been foolish to think that maybe Kyle wanted to be a family, the three of them. Without Landon and Lexie. But even as she had the thought, she couldn't imagine her life without Landon.

"I don't think that's how it works." Morgan started walking again, and Kyle got in step with her.

"Emma is my child too."

Here we go. Her mother had warned her this might happen, that Kyle could pull the legal card. She'd fiercely defended him and said he wouldn't. "So, are you going to fight me for custody now?" *You can try.* She looked back at Landon, knowing that wasn't even a remote possibility. But her blood ran cold just hearing the possessive implication in Kyle's voice.

"I would never do that." He stopped and faced her again. "Emma doesn't even know me. I've spent barely more than a few minutes here and there with her since I've been here. My entire world is upside down. I want to know my daughter. I want to know her, Morgan!" Kyle lowered his gaze, and Morgan touched his arm, but he flinched and jerked away from her, then looked her in the eyes again. "I want to know her, Morgan."

She decided not to correct him on the name issue as tears pooled in the corners of his eyes.

"I'm going to give my daughter my stem cells, and I'm blessed and honored to be able to do that." He blinked his eyes a few times. "Then your bodyguard over there…" He nodded toward Landon and Emma."…will send me packing. And you'll fly back to wherever it is you came from."

Well, not exactly. Niihau was a short flight or boat ride from Honolulu. Morgan couldn't find any words of comfort.

"Will I get a graduation picture? A wedding picture? Will I know that she's okay and well?" Kyle blinked his eyes a few times and warded off any tears, but Morgan could tell he was struggling not to break down. "And don't tell me that life isn't fair. I get that. Totally. I lost my dad. I lost you. And now I'm going to lose Emma too."

Morgan reached for him again, but he took a step backward. "No. Just don't."

"Kyle, what can I do?" She eased forward, and he didn't back up this time." Tell me. What can I do to make this easier for you?"

He raised both his shoulders, then dropped them slowly as he blew out a long gust of air. "I have no idea. I'm no match for your dad or your CIA boyfriend."

"He's not my boyfriend." Morgan looked at Landon and Emma growing closer. Landon was carrying Emma now, which meant her daughter was already getting tired.

"Well, he used to be, and maybe he should be now. Emma needs a father, and if I can't be it, then maybe it should be Landon. She obviously loves him." He shook his head. "I don't even know how to feel. I want to have a bond with Emma, and I want to love her—just not too much. That probably sounds awful, but a guy can only take so much heartache. And I might have another big one coming when I get home and face Lexie. She has nothing to do with any of this, but I can't even imagine how much she's suffering."

Morgan forcibly pulled Kyle into her arms and held him. He cupped his hand behind her head and eased her cheek onto his chest. "Tell me what to do, Kyle."

He eased away. "I don't know." Kyle dabbed at his eyes before any tears spilled, and he smiled as Landon and Emma got closer. Landon set Emma down in front of Kyle.

"Mr. Kyle, are you crying?" Emma pushed her white sunglasses up on her head and walked closer to him. Kyle squatted down in the sand and faced her as she cupped his cheeks in her small hands. Morgan held her breath. Even at five, Emma had always been sensitive and compassionate. Something she'd gotten from Kyle.

"Not really crying, but I think I need a hug," Kyle said barely above a whisper.

Emma released her hold on his cheeks and threw her tiny arms around Kyle. "Mommy says when times get tough, we put our worries into a big giant bubble and blow them to God. He catches the bubbles in heaven and takes care of everything." She stepped out of the hug and scrunched her face into a serious expression, her lips pressed together in a thin smile. "Do you want us to make a bubble for your troubles?"

Poor Kyle. He was having trouble maintaining much composure, but Morgan could see him still trying to keep any tears in check.

"I think that's a great idea." Kyle stood up, smiled at Morgan, then he and Emma emulated a big circle and blew the invisible bubble filled with worries and prayers to heaven.

"Maybe you two want to take a walk together," Landon said, a slight smile on his face, as he glanced at Morgan.

That most likely meant that Landon wanted to talk to Morgan alone. When Emma reached for Kyle's hand and they started down the beach, Morgan brought a hand to her chest. Emma was smiling and chattering away. She prayed her daughter would remember the rules about what not to say.

After they were out of earshot, Landon said, "We need to talk."

"If you want to talk about me hugging Kyle, he was just upset. Nothing more to it."

Landon hung his head for a few moments, then looked back up at her and sighed." Mia, I'm not going to be that person. I love you and Emma enough to want you to be happy, whether I'm in the picture or not. I've told you that. If you choose to be with Kyle, I'm not going to fight it." He gently held both of her arms, the waves breaking closer to their feet and seemingly louder than before.

Morgan gazed into his eyes. She opened her mouth to speak, but nothing came out.

"I know you're confused. This is a bizarre situation, and I really and truly feel badly for Kyle. And I've heard repeatedly from you—and even your mother—that you're scared to let anyone get too close for fear of losing them again. I need to know if that's really what caused you to break up with me, or is the reason walking down the beach with Emma? I need to know that, and you need to be fair to yourself, me… and Kyle. Because, I'm here to tell you, if you'll let me into your heart again, I promise to never leave you, no matter what." He took a breath, looked out across the water, and looked back at Morgan. "I would always figure out a way for us to stay together. But I don't want to be a second choice if you're going to spend your life harboring feelings for another man."

Morgan looked down the beach at Kyle holding Emma's hand, her daughter slowly walking alongside him and smiling. Morgan looked on for a few seconds before she wrapped her arms around Landon's waist and buried her head in his chest.

"Mia, I love you and Emma with all my heart." He kissed her forehead.

"I know you do," she said softly in the comfort of his protective embrace. She snuck another look at father and daughter. The man she'd once loved, the daughter they'd created, and the possibilities that loomed before her now.

Life had never seemed more confusing.

Chapter Ten

Lexie sat on her couch staring at the television that wasn't even on. She kicked her feet up on the coffee table and slouched into the cushions. Life as she knew it had ended. It was a dramatic thought, but everything she'd believed in was in question. She prayed continuously to hear from Kyle, but she'd become so physically ill from worry that her parents had tried to talk her into moving back home, which wasn't an option for Lexie. That would mean she'd accepted that Kyle wasn't coming back, and she didn't believe that.

Kyle's mother called every day, and Lexie knew Diana was worried sick, but the woman had a job to go to every day, so that was a distraction. Lexie was off for the summer, but even if she hadn't been, not even teaching could have distracted her from the hundreds of scenarios she'd dreamed up about what could have happened to Kyle. She closed her eyes.

God, if Kyle isn't meant to be with me, I'll live with that. But I just pray with all my heart that he is okay. Please God, keep Your loving arms around him.

She reached into the bag of Cheetos next to her on the couch, forcing herself to eat a few, then she lay her head back against the couch, wishing sleep would come and knowing it wouldn't. Her lids were heavy but they snapped open when her phone rang. She hurried to her purse on the kitchen table, found her phone, and almost fell over when she saw the 808 area code.

"Kyle, is that you?" She held her breath and waited but the phone went dead. With shaky fingers and a trembling lip, she hit Redial. A man answered on the first ring.

"Sir, I believe you just called me. Are you with Kyle Brossmann by any chance?" *Maybe it's his kidnapper.* She held her breath. "Please don't hang up."

"Um, I'm sorry for the call. I must have hit this number stored in my phone by mistake."

"I—I'm looking for someone. I think he's… missing. And I received a call from a Hawaii area code over a week ago. This is the second call, but I guess it could be a coincidence." Lexie thought about the cufflink and decided to press on. "Can you tell me how you think you ended up with my phone number?"

"I'm sorry. I have no idea. Where are you calling from?"

Lexie shook all over as her heart thumped in her chest. He didn't sound like a kidnapper. "I'm in Texas."

"No, I'm sorry. I don't know anyone in Texas, but I wish you all the best finding your friend."

"Thank you."

"Uh, wait a minute."

Lexie brought a hand to her chest. "Did you think of something?"

"Yeah, I did. I was in the men's room, and a young man asked to borrow my phone, said he was from Houston and needed to call his girlfriend. I handed him the phone, but I don't think the call even went through when he handed it back. Another man came out of the bathroom, and honestly the guy who borrowed the phone seemed a little spooked. He handed me the phone back and said never mind."

Lexie sat in a kitchen chair and tried to steady her breathing. "Can you tell me where in Hawaii you are?"

"Honolulu. If your friend is missing, have you called the authorities?"

"Yes, but they didn't feel there was enough to warrant a Missing Persons Report." Although she hadn't checked back with the police in a few days.

"Can I ask you one other thing, please? Can you tell me how far Niihau Island is from Honolulu?"

"I'm surprised you'd even know about Niihau Island. Many of the locals don't even know about that place. It's referred to as the Forbidden Isle or the Forbidden Island. There aren't many people living there, and until recently, only friends and family of the residents were allowed to visit. I think there are a few tourist boats that might go there these days. There's not even any electricity there, just solar power and generators."

Sounds like the perfect place to hold someone hostage. Lexie's mind was racing. "Is it far from Honolulu?"

"Honestly, I've never been there. You can take a boat or a helicopter, but I'm not too sure how long it takes. They've got Navy personnel out there and some government offices I believe. Biggest thing Niihau is known for are the lei pupa, their shell leis. They go for thousands of dollars, I've heard."

"If I text you a picture of the man who asked to borrow your phone, do you think you'd recognize him?" Lexie still had her hand on her heart.

"Maybe. I've slept since then. But you're welcome to send it."

Lexie maneuvered to her Texts, found a picture of Kyle, and said, "Don't hang up. I'm sending it now."

"I'm not sure I know how to check a text message while I'm on the phone, so if I lose you, I'll call you back."

Lexie waited.

"I got it. And yep, that's the kid from the restroom."

Lexie burst into tears. "Thank you," she said barely above a whisper.

"You're welcome. Godspeed to you. I hope you find your friend."

Lexie wanted to cry for a long time. But there was no time for that.

Kyle slowed his stride when Emma did. "Are you tired? Do you want me to carry you?"

Emma frowned. "No."

"Oh, uh...I saw Landon carrying you, so I just thought maybe... "

"That's different. He's my bodyguard." She looked up at Kyle. "But I want him to be my daddy. I've never had one, but Landon says it's up to Mommy."

Kyle felt a blow to his gut, but even worse to his heart. "So you must think Landon is a really good guy?"

"Yes." She smiled as her pace picked up a little. "He's strong too."

They walked quietly, but it wasn't long before Emma slowed down again. Kyle glanced over his shoulder at Morgan and Landon—hugging. Swallowing hard, he stopped walking when Emma squatted down to pick up a shell. Once they were moving again, Kyle took a deep breath.

"Do you get to walk on the beach a lot where you live?" He held his breath. What kind of person tries to trick a five-year-old? *A desperate father.*

Emma didn't look up, but just shrugged as she pushed her little, white sunglasses up on her nose. Then she held up a small shell for Kyle to see.

"It's pretty." He leaned in to have a closer look at the white shell, then Emma closed her hand around it and picked up the pace. His mind was full of questions, five year's worth, but Kyle didn't know where to begin, and his stomach was doing flips again, so that left him fearful he might hurl right there on the beach.

Kyle slowed down. "Emma…"

She stopped and looked up at him through her sunglasses. He squatted down, gently eased off her shades, and gazed into her deep blue eyes. Kyle didn't want to love her, but the emotion must be factored into the parental gene, which had reared its head over the past week. And now, he couldn't imagine leaving her. He wanted to tell his mother about Emma, scream it from the rooftops, tell Lexie, and fight Landon and Morgan to see her. But as he stared into this precious child's eyes, he knew he wouldn't do any of that. He'd die to keep her safe.

He saw Landon and Morgan out of the corner of his eye, but he didn't care. Time was running out. After he gave Emma his stem cells, he'd get shipped home, even though Emma had a long road to recovery ahead. He couldn't pull his gaze away from his daughter. *How can I have you in my life?*

"Everything okay?" Morgan asked as she stood next to Landon.

Kyle considered his options. He could fight hard to win Morgan back so they could all be a family. *But Lexie.* He couldn't imagine his life without her. Could he sacrifice Lexie to be with Emma?

He pushed back thin strands of golden hair from Emma's face. "Do you know what a beautiful little girl you are?" Kyle struggled to keep his voice from cracking.

Emma nodded and smiled as she pointed to Landon. "That's what he says too."

Kyle didn't look at the man who would most likely continue raising Emma, or at the least, be a huge part of her life. "I know you understand why I'm here, right?"

Emma nodded again. "To give me some of your stem cells to make me better."

Kyle took in another deep breath. "That's right. And wherever you go, you'll always have a part of me with you. And wherever I am, I'll always be praying you're okay."

Emma's bottom lip turned under as she gazed into Kyle's eyes. "I should give you something too."

You already have. "I think a hug would do."

Emma wrapped her arms around Kyle's neck and squeezed. He pulled her closer, swallowed back tears, and couldn't bring himself to let go of her, even when she started to ease away. *I love you, Emma. Feel my love.*

He finally let her out of his bear hug and put her sunglasses back on her. She handed him the shell. "Here," she said softly in her delicate voice. "You can have this."

Kyle held out his palm, and Emma dropped the small shell in his hand. Then she turned to Morgan, smiled, and walked to Landon. "I'm tired," she said. "Can you carry me?"

Landon scooped her into his arms. "Yep. Why don't we go find something to drink, and we'll let your mom and Mr. Kyle talk."

Emma waved to Kyle over Landon's shoulder. After they were out of earshot, Kyle sat down in the sand. More like folded into a lump in the sand. Morgan knelt down beside him.

"I can't believe you've done this to me." He heard how selfish it sounded the moment the words slipped from his lips. Clutching the small shell in one hand, he tapped his chest a few times. "I thought I'd die when you just vanished." Glancing down the beach at Landon and Emma again, his daughter waved. He raised his hand and tried to smile. "But now this. How am I going to say goodbye to her, Morgan? How? Tell me how, because I'm not sure I'll have the strength."

She lowered her head and put a hand on his leg. "Kyle, if you're wanting me to tell you I'm sorry for bringing you here, I can't do that." She looked up at him as tears started down her face. "You are saving our daughter's life. And I know it's at a great personal cost for you. I know this." She shrugged. "I don't know how to make things right. All I know is that because of you, our daughter should live a full life after the transplant. As long as there aren't any unexpected problems—and the doctors don't think there will be—then Emma will go on to lead a good life."

Kyle dabbed at his eyes, something he'd been doing a lot of. Part of him just wanted to let it all go and sob for hours. Another tear slid down Morgan's cheek.

"Do you have any idea how much I loved you?" Kyle held her gaze as he gently ran his thumb along her moist cheek.

She put her hand over his and pressed it closer to her cheek. "And I loved you." She lowered his hand, but squeezed it. "I still do."

Kyle still wasn't sure if he was going to throw up. He wasn't sure if it was from the medications he'd taken or the effort it was taking to suppress his emotions. He was sure he'd never watered up this much in his life. He pulled Morgan to him and held her while she cried as he struggled to keep his own tears at bay. When it seemed they had both exhausted all the emotion that had built up over the past five years, he looked at her, kissed her on the cheek, and leaned away.

"Do you love Landon?"

Morgan was sure that Kyle had been leading up to tell her that he was going to stay here, which would have complicated her life in several ways, no matter the emotional tug of war going on in her heart. "I love you both."

"We both love what we had." He nodded past her at Emma and Landon, who were almost out of sight, but Morgan knew Landon would never be completely out of sight. "And we love Emma," he said." "You know what I'm asking you. Do you love Landon, enough to make a life with him? I don't understand why you broke up with him. If he's not the one, then—"

"I thought you were the one." She glared at him. "And then I thought Landon was the one. But every time I allowed myself to be completely in love with him, I'd think of you, the way it all happened. I couldn't bear that again."

"Morgan." He shook his head. "Sorry, I'm never going to get used to you as Mia. Anyway, first of all, I don't know why you think that. He's CIA. He's probably the only guy in the world that won't get forced out of your life. If you love him, and he loves you, then maybe…" Kyle shrugged.

"What if he dies?" Morgan held her breath. The thought horrified her. "Every day for the past year, I've worried that Emma wouldn't get better. It's the kind of love that would make you easily die for another person. I started feeling that way about Landon. I loved him so much it hurt. I don't want to love that way. There's too much risk."

One side of Kyle's mouth curved up a little. "I felt that way about Lexie in the beginning, afraid I'd love her too much. Then lose her."

"I bet she's going crazy not knowing where you are. I wish things could have played out in a way that made things easier on you."

He was quiet for a while. Morgan was sure his emotions clawed and scratched at his heart the way hers were.

"How am I going to say goodbye to you and Emma again?" he asked again.

Morgan forced a smile. Even after all these years, she couldn't stand to see Kyle hurting this way. "With thoughts of getting home to Lexie."

"Lexie," he said in a whisper as his gaze drifted out to the ocean.

"Landon," she said softly, her stare parallel with his out to sea.

"Emma loves him," Kyle said a few moments later. "He would be a good father to her."

Morgan nodded. "He would." She reached for Kyle's hand, and for a long while, they both sat in the sand, watching the waves roll in, crashing not far from them, then the surf quieted, and the sea became calm.

Chapter Eleven

Kyle waited as a nurse took his blood pressure in the outpatient wing of the hospital. He was surprised that no one had come to be with him while he gave up his stem cells. Granted, it was an easy procedure, and he'd already been cleared to go home, but still. Maybe this was the beginning of the detachment phase. He'd already been told that his stem cells would be frozen until Emma was at her optimum health-wise.

"Pretty bracelet." He eyed the nurse's bracelet, almost exactly the same as the unusual one Morgan had worn the day at the restaurant.

"Thanks. I don't usually wear jewelry to work." She shrugged as she peeled off the blood pressure cuff from Kyle's arm. "But today is my birthday, so I made an exception. A bunch of us old ladies are going to kick up our heels after work." She chuckled. "Or try to."

Kyle smiled. "Happy birthday. I saw someone else wearing a bracelet like that. The shells are really pretty, different."

The woman held up her wrist. "This was a gift from my daughter and her husband. The shells come from Niihau Island and can't be found anywhere else in the world."

Kyle sat up on the bed and hung his legs over the side as his eyes opened wider. *Really?* "I've heard of Maui, Kauai, and some of the others, but not Niihau."

"The forbidden isle, we call it. Not everyone knows about it." She shook her head. "I couldn't live there. They don't even have electricity, just solar power. It's pretty detached from the rest of the islands."

Kyle wished he could get Lexie a bracelet like that, but he felt sure it was going to take more than a bracelet to get back into his fiancée's good graces. And he couldn't help but recall what Morgan said about her mother, that Patty had collected the shells where they lived.

"Have you seen Mia or any of the others this morning, the people that are usually here with Emma?"

"No, I haven't. But the weather is awful. It's been raining since I woke up this morning."

Kyle figured they didn't want to get Emma out in the rain, but Morgan could have come. Or Neal—*Alex*. Or Patty. Someone.

He tucked away any hurt feelings, and once he was cleared to leave, he hailed a cab to his hotel, wondering what the timeline was on his departure. He'd hoped that Emma would have the transplant before he left, but he could understand the doctors wanting her to be at her best.

But when he walked into his hotel room, he saw that the timeline for his departure had already been established. His small red suitcase was packed, and there was a letter on the bed.

Dear Kyle,

Saying goodbye again is too much to bear for all of us, and Emma wouldn't understand a tearful farewell. Please forgive me for this—and for everything we've all done to cause you pain. I hope you can feel joy and peace knowing you will be saving our daughter's life. The doctors have reiterated over and over again that fate had a hand in all of this. I know better, though. God has His hand on all of us, especially Emma.

"Joy and peace? Are you kidding me?" Kyle sat down on the bed and reminded himself to breathe.

A part of me will always love you. But Landon holds my heart, and I need to let go of my fears. You were right about Landon being a good father to Emma.

There is so much I could say right now, Kyle. But I know that there are no words to ease your pain. This is the life that God planned for us, and we have to make the best of it. I will think of you every time I gaze into our beautiful daughter's blue eyes.

I wish you all good things in life, and I pray that you and Lexie will live a wonderful life together filled with love and happiness. There is a commercial plane ticket home in your suitcase.

With love always,

Mia (and Landon, Dad, Mom, and Emma)

Kyle set the letter on the bed, folded his hands on his lap, and thought about his situation. He could sit here and cry or fight for his right to be with Emma. *I am not defeated. Yet.*

Lexie exited the boat at Niihau Island and wandered away from the other six passengers, despite the warnings that she could be in a heap of trouble with the locals if she was caught just wandering around on an island that didn't look kindly on outsiders. But as she rubbed the cufflink in her hand, she prayed that God would lead her to Kyle. The cufflink was the only clue she had.

She glanced down at her hand, void of her engagement ring. She'd pawned it to get a plane ticket, including a return flight. But she didn't know how she'd leave here without Kyle. After a full day of travel, she'd stayed in Kauai overnight, then booked a ticket on one of the few tours that came to Niihau. One maxed out credit card later, she fought the panic taking hold of her. She'd just spent a fortune based on a cufflink and a couple of phone calls. Not the Hawaii trip she would have imagined.

She waded in the bluest water she'd ever seen, getting further and further away from the boat she'd arrived on. The island had all the elements of a Hawaiian paradise at first glance, with the white sanded beach stretching as far as she could see. The biggest difference; it looked almost deserted if not for the boat with it's few passengers in the distance. The tour she'd paid for was for a half a day. There was no lodging, or even a restaurant on Niihau.

Despite her parents' pleading not to go, she'd made the trip anyway. After two flights and eight hours in the air to think, she'd come up with just about every scenario possible. Kyle had been kidnapped and was being held on this remote island. Why wasn't there a ransom call? Or Kyle had truly gotten cold feet and decided to get as far away from her as possible. *Nope*. She didn't believe that. Or another fear—that there was someone else, and they'd snuck off to get married and live in Hawaii. *Nope.* She didn't buy that either.

But a calling larger than her own thoughts and conscience had led her to Hawaii and onto the boat to this remote island. She eased away from the water and started her trek further down the unpopulated beach. After a while, she slung off her backpack and looked around. There was a village on the island. And she was going to find it.

Lexie bowed her head, put her palms together, and prayed.

Kyle sat down on his red suitcase near the water's edge. He'd tried to call Lexie a dozen times before he'd taken a boat to Niihau Island, but his phone still wasn't working. He'd tried from his hotel and a nearby restaurant on Kauai also, and no answer. Had she forgotten about him over the past couple of weeks? *No way.*

He was thankful the weather had cleared up and skeptical that Morgan, Emma and her family were here. But after he'd thought for a while, the only thing he had to go on was origin of Morgan's bracelet.

A little research later, and he confirmed what the nurse told him about Niihua Island. A long shot, but it sounded like a good place to shack up if you were in hiding. But he'd asked everyone he'd run into in the small village of Puuwai if they knew Mia, Alex, Patty, Emma, or Landon and Sean. Most just shook their head and kept going. One lady had told him to get off their island.

He only had a half a day to play detective. That was all the time an outsider was allowed on Niihau. And so far, the trip had been a bust. He sat on his suitcase, which he'd optimistically carted through the village hoping he'd find Morgan and Emma. Now he just felt silly. He stared out over the deep blue water, and attempted to pray.

God, I don't even know where to start...

He closed his eyes, but movement to his left snapped him to attention as a woman approached him. At that moment, he was sure they'd given him something at the hospital to make him go crazy. Maybe a drug to erase his memories or to make him hallucinate. It was a wild speculation from watching too many movies, but there was no way Lexie could be walking toward him.

As he stood up, his legs carried him toward someone, and when he got close enough to recognize his hallucination, he ran to her, threw his arms around her, and they fell to the sand in each other's arms.

And for the first time since all of this started, Kyle let go of the tears he'd fought to bottle up and sobbed.

Lexie kept her arms around Kyle as he cried, and it wasn't long before she cried along with him. Whatever had happened, he was racked with grief, and she couldn't stand seeing him in so much pain. But her own relief that she'd found him was enough to rattle her own resolve, and despite the torment, she could feel the love radiating between them.

When they both gained some composure, Kyle told her about his heartbreaking adventure, and Lexie cried the entire time.

"I thought for sure they were here. I felt called to come here, but now I know I was called here to run into you, not to find Emma." Kyle clutched both of Lexie's hands as he recounted the events. Even after they'd sat up, he'd never let go of her. "How'd you get here?"

"I chartered a private boat." Lexie tried to control her trembling bottom lip. Now was surely the worse possible time to tell Kyle her secret, but she didn't know how much longer she could hold it in.

Kyle lifted her left hand and rubbed the top of her hand. "Lexie, where's your ring?"

"I pawned it before I left," she said through tears. "But I'll get it back."

"Oh, Lexie." Kyle lowered his head, shaking it. "No, I'll get it back. This is a trip you shouldn't have had to make." He gently cupped her cheek with his hand. "You're sunburned," he said.

Lexie wasn't sure how long they'd been sitting on the beach. Long enough that the tide had come up and they'd had to move back. "You are too."

Kyle stood up, pulling Lexie with him. "Let's find some shade and see if we can find something to drink."

They finally detached from each other. Lexie knew Kyle well, but she was wise enough to know that there was no way she could truly understand what he must be feeling. This was bound to play out emotionally, for both of them, for a long time. But for now, she praised God that Kyle was okay and that she'd found him.

An older woman with gray hair and a broom in her hand stepped outside a small house and walked toward them. "Do you have business here?" The dark skinned woman looked like she'd lived her entire life in the sun, with wrinkles that webbed across a thin face, spilled down her neck, and ran the length of her arms. Her dark hair hung long as she squinted her eyes and brought a hand to her forehead.

Lexie cleared her throat, knowing they both must look a mess with their swollen eyes and still covered in sand. "Um, we're looking for someone." She glanced at Kyle.

"The Smith family," he said. "Mia, Alex, Patty, and Emma." His voice cracked when he said his daughter's name. Lexie's heart broke for him, and she said another prayer.

The old woman pointed to her left. "Two blocks down, the big house with all the solar panels."

Kyle nodded, and he and Lexie headed in that direction.

"Wow. You must look more trusting than me," he said after they'd taken a few steps. "I couldn't get anyone to help me."

The closer they got, the faster Kyle walked. As the house came into view, Kyle let go of her hand, sprinted up the steps, and went straight to the window.

Lexie hurried to his side as the butterflies in her stomach fluttered and spun.

"Thank God," he said as he bent at the waist. "The last time this happened, I showed up at an empty house." Kyle knocked on the door. When no one answered, he knocked again. And again.

"They must not be home." Lexie's knees were weak. The entire trip had been surreal, but standing here on the porch with Kyle, knowing now that he has a daughter, and possibly about to be face to face with the woman he loved before her... she felt dizzy. She reached for Kyle's arm just as the door swung open.

A woman with salt and pepper hair and wearing an apron eyed them. "Can I help you?" It obviously wasn't anyone who knew Kyle, and the woman was holding a bottle of Windex.

"I'm looking for the family who lives here. The Smith family. Mia, Alex, Patty, and Emma."

"I'm sorry. They left the island this morning." The woman tipped her head to one side as she looked Kyle up and down before shifting her gaze to Lexie and doing the same thing.

"Do you know when they'll be back?" Kyle was trembling. Lexie reached her arm around his waist.

"They're not coming back. They moved. Left here for good. They'd rented the place furnished, and the landlord hired me to come clean and ready the place to lease again. This is the only house for rent on the island, so it will move quickly."

Kyle bent at the waist, and Lexie did her best to keep him on his feet. "I can't believe this is happening again."

Lexie kept her arm around him as his body shook with more tears. Lexie thanked the woman for her time as she led Kyle off the porch.

Chapter Twelve

Morgan buckled Emma into her seat by the window, as requested. Landon was on the other side of Morgan, and Morgan's parents and Sean were in the three seats in front of them. "I don't remember the last time I was on a commercial flight," Morgan said to Landon.

"It wasn't our first choice. Your father said our private jet was cleared to go, but there was a suspicious odor that the pilot couldn't identify, so your dad wanted to play it safe but still get off the island quickly." Landon spoke in a whisper.

Morgan reached for his hand, glancing at his wrist, and having a random thought. "I haven't seen you wear the cufflinks I gave you in a long time. You used to wear them even with your casual shirts."

Landon sighed, frowning. "I lost one. I was going to tell you, but I kept thinking it would show up."

"I would buy new ones for you, but they wouldn't be from Niihau Island. I'm guessing we won't see that place again." She paused, realizing she'd miss the quaint village with its friendly, if not a bit aloof, residents. "You're sure everything is okay with the transferring of Kyle's frozen stem cells?" She closed her eyes and leaned her head back for a few moments as the engine on the plane roared, preparing to take off.

"Yep. It's all being handled."

Morgan glanced at Emma, who was blissfully unaware of her circumstances. "The doctors said she is okay for now, but she'll need the stem cells soon." She sighed, then turned her head toward Landon and spoke softly. "I can't believe we did this to Kyle. Again."

"I know. I feel badly about it too. But there was just too much chatter again, and your father wouldn't have made this hasty move, especially with Emma sick, unless he felt strongly that you were all in danger."

"I'm so tired of living like this, Landon. Is this how it will be for Emma all of her life too?" Her mouth was almost in his ear as the plane started to taxi.

"No. I'm going to figure something out, so that both of you aren't always on the run. Unless the situation works itself out in another way."

Morgan turned to Emma, wondering if her daughter would be assigned a new name. And who would Morgan be this time? "You ready to take off?" she asked Emma. Her daughter had flown plenty of times, but always on a private plane.

"Yes." Emma smiled and nodded her head. "I'm ready."

Morgan slid her fingernail into the locket around her neck and eased it open. She stared for a long few seconds at Landon and Emma's picture inside, their faces pressed cheek to cheek. Deep down, she'd known all along that she would be with Landon.

She leaned her head back and closed her eyes again. Her heart cried for Kyle. But she'd done one thing differently this time, left a silver lining in an unbearable situation. Later, she'd tell Landon what she'd done, but for now, she planned to keep it to herself.

Kyle felt like he was in an entirely different episode of The Twilight Zone, wondering how he was going to recover from this. *Thank God for Lexie*. He squeezed her hand. "We should be landing in about an hour," he said.

They'd finally taken the boat to Kauai, then traveled to Honolulu, and went straight to the airport. Combining what little money they had left, they paid the fee to change Lexie's plane ticket and got her on the same flight as Kyle to LAX, then Houston. And a guy about Kyle's age had swapped seats with him on the second flight so he could sit next to Lexie. He didn't want to be away from her, even on the plane. She'd already said she never gave up on their love, that she knew he didn't write the email, and that she loved him more than ever before. But he knew Lexie well enough to know that something big was on her mind.

"Are you wondering if I ever thought about staying? I mean, if I thought about staying with Morgan and Emma?" Kyle held tightly to her hand, to assure her that he wouldn't have left her for them. But he planned to be honest too.

She laid her head on his shoulder, avoiding his eyes. In a whisper, she said, "It crossed my mind. She was your first love. And the mother of your child."

Kyle took a deep breath. "I thought about it." He felt her tense against his shoulder, and he nudged her until she locked eyes with him. "And there will always be a place in my heart for Morgan, and of course for Emma. But even when I tried to picture a life with them, Lexie... I couldn't picture my life without you."

Tears trickled down her cheeks. "I have something to tell you, and I don't want there to be anything between us."

He stopped breathing. "What?"

"I—I…" She squeezed her eyes closed as another round of tears trailed her cheeks.

"Lexie, what is it?" Kyle was desperate to know, but terrified too. He wasn't sure how much more he could handle.

"I can't have children." Lexie locked eyes with him. "So maybe you didn't make the right choice."

Kyle's heart pounded in his chest as he processed what she was saying.

She swiped at her eyes, trying to whisper as she spoke. "I'm sorry. I'm so sorry. I should have told you sooner. I was going to tell you before we got married, in case you wanted to back out. There's a long medical explanation, but I was in a car accident when I was younger, and it left me barren. My parents have been pushing me to tell you, and I was going to, and then I got scared, and…" She could barely breathe, she was crying so hard.

Kyle was glad it was dark and most passengers were sleeping. He searched for words of comfort, but he was speechless.

"You might have chosen to stay with them if you had known, and I'm so sorry."

"Lexie." He cupped her cheeks in his hands and kissed her on the mouth. "It wouldn't have mattered. I will always have a special place in my heart for Morgan, and I feel shattered about Emma." He paused, swallowing hard. "But I never want to be without you. I love you. Somehow, we're going to get through all this."

"But, what about having a family?" She buried her head against his shoulder again, but he eased her away and found her troubled gaze.

"We are each other's family, and God will set us on whatever path He deems right. As long as we walk the walk, live the right way, and hold steady to our faith, we're going to be fine."

Kyle's eyes widened. *Did I just say that?* The Lord was surely on the plane with them, feeding Kyle hope that all would be well, even though the pressure in his chest felt like an elephant was sitting on him. He was so stressed out, depressed, sad, happy, and thankful, all at the same time. It was no wonder his chest hurt. But then he remembered something.

"Awe, man. I forgot to take my pill this morning. Of all days." He unhooked his seatbelt and slipped quietly into the aisle, then opened the hatch above them. His small suitcase had barely fit, and he had to struggle to get it down.

"My suitcase," Lexie whispered from her seat.

"I figured it was. I grabbed the first one I found." He said a quick prayer that whoever had so neatly packed his things hadn't forgotten the pill bottle in the bathroom. And he'd been way too upset to even check before he'd left the hotel.

"Ah. Got it," he whispered to Lexie, handing her the bottle so he could stow his suitcase again. He eased back into his seat and twisted the lid. When he tipped the bottle, four pills fell into his palm—and a piece of paper. He took one capsule, put the other three back in the bottle, then unfolded a tiny note. His heart thudded wildly against his chest. There was only one person he knew who would leave him a message like this.

> *Kyle,*
>
> *This was the only way I knew to get word to you without anyone knowing. I promise you with all my heart, I will find a way for you to be in Emma's life. Once again, I'm sorry. This is my promise to you.*
>
> *Morgan*

Kyle was sure he had no tears left. His world had been rocked, spun, shattered, repaired, blessed, and rebuilt. He handed the note to Lexie and covered his face with one hand. After a few seconds, he opened his eyes and saw her smiling in the dimly lit plane.

"A message in a bottle," he whispered softly.

Lexie grabbed his hand, kissed the top of it, and smiled again. "What a whirlwind all of this has been, but I have to believe that everything is going to be okay. With his free hand, he touched the shell he'd strung and put around his neck, the one Emma had given him at the beach. "I'll be praying that Morgan keeps her promise."

"Me too." Kyle pulled Lexie's face to his, kissed her softly on the lips, and as she rested her head on his shoulder again, he begged God to keep Morgan and Emma safe, and for Emma to be healthy.

Then he prayed hard that Morgan would keep her promise. And that God would hear his prayer.

Epilogue

Fifteen years later…

Kyle kept his eyes looking forward, even though it was hard not to look at the beautiful bride walking next to him. His right arm intertwined with her left arm as they both took slow steps on shaky legs. He wasn't sure who was keeping who steady on their feet. Maybe they were holding each other up.

Guests rose to stand in the church where Kyle had attended worship as a child. Kyle praised God for allowing him to be a part of this fabulous journey. Even the priest had a smile stretched across his face as they approached the altar.

"Who gives this woman to be with this man?" Father Griggs asked.

Kyle glanced at Morgan, seated on the front row to their left. "Her mother and I." Then he smiled at Lexie, on the pew behind Morgan. "Along with her stepmother, Lexie."

Kyle's mother smiled broadly from where she was seated next to Morgan's parents. Somehow Patty had seemed to stay endlessly young, but Alex—the name he still used—had aged way past his years, and Kyle assumed the man's job might have played a big role in that.

When Kyle turned to Emma, he lifted her veil, and all of his memories from the past fifteen years bubbled to the surface in a euphoria of happiness. "You've never looked more beautiful," he whispered as he kissed her on the cheek. "I love you to the moon and back." A phrase that he now shared with Lexie and Emma.

She smiled. "I love you, too, Dad. To the moon and back." She glanced at Morgan, then back at Kyle. "I wish Landon was here," she said in a whisper.

"Me too. But he's smiling from heaven."

Emma's blue eyes twinkled as she took a deep breath.

Kyle's gaze drifted in Morgan's direction. He could still recall the conversation they'd had in Hawaii, when Morgan said, "What if he dies?"—in reference to Landon. A fear that came to pass much too early for her husband.

Landon been gone almost five years, but he'd been just as much a father to Emma as Kyle, maybe more. Lexie had told him once, that a child could never have too much love, and they'd all shared in Emma's life.

Kyle handed his daughter's hand to the man who would be responsible for her well-being from now on. Shane was a good man, and Kyle knew God had His hand on this, the same way He'd kept His hand on all of them over the years.

Morgan had kept her promise, but ultimately it had been Landon who closed the door on the case that had kept Morgan's family in danger. It should have been his time to enjoy a normal life, but colon cancer took him way too young.

Kyle returned to his seat. He glanced at Morgan and smiled. She had her arm around her twin thirteen-year-old boys, who looked more and more like Landon every year. Kyle turned to his left when one of his own boys poked him in the arm.

"What is it?" he asked Zackary, who was also celebrating his sixth birthday today.

"Emma looks pretty," he said, smiling with a big hole in his mouth where one of his teeth should be.

"Yes, she does." Kyle turned to Lexie and winked. Then he scanned their entire crew. All five of them. As it turned out, the doctors had been more than a little wrong about Lexie. Or maybe they'd been right, but God chose to gift them five precious miracles.

He tuned back into the ceremony, smiling, as Emma professed her love to Shane.

Be blessed in all that you do, Emma. As I am a blessed man to know you and love you.

A Tide Worth
Turning

"Masterful storytelling."
Kelly Long, Zebra Books bestseller

a
Surf's Up
novella

BETH WISEMAN

**Grab another novella in the
Surf's Up series!**

About the Author

Beth Wiseman is the best-selling author of the Daughters of the Promise series and the Land of Canaan series. Having sold over 1.5 million books, her novels have held spots on the ECPA (Evangelical Christian Publishers Association) Bestseller List and the CBA (Christian Book Association) Bestseller List. She was the recipient of the prestigious Carol Award in 2011 and 2013.

She is a three-time winner of the Inspirational Readers Choice Award, and an INSPY Award winner. In 2013 she took home the coveted Holt Medallion. Her first book in the Land of Canaan series—*Seek Me With All Your Heart*—was selected as the 2011 Women of Faith Book of the Year. Beth and her husband are empty nesters enjoying country life in South Central Texas.

Other books by Beth Wiseman

The Daughters of the Promise series (Amish)
Plain Perfect   *Plain Paradise*
Plain Pursuit   *Plain Proposal*
Plain Promise   *Plain Peace*

Land of Canaan series (Amish)
Seek Me With All Your Heart
The Wonder of Your Love
His Love Endures Forever

Amish Secrets series
Her Brother's Keeper
Love Bears All Things

Women's Fiction
Need You Now
The House that Love Built
The Promise

Surf's Up Novellas
A Tide Worth Turning
Message In A Bottle

Visit www.bethwiseman.com for more information about Beth and her books. Visit Fans of Beth Wiseman on Facebook.

Acknowledgments

To my family and friends, another big thank you for your continued support as I travel on this amazing journey. Special thanks to my fabulous husband, Patrick, for being patient and tolerant when I'm up against a deadline, especially when it's a 'fend for yourself' dinner night.

Audrey Wick, it's an honor to dedicate this novella to you, and I do so with much appreciation. A huge thanks for the time and level of professionalism you gave to this project. Not only were your revisions spot on, but it was also a joy to work with you. I value our friendship, and I'm your biggest cheerleader when it comes to your own writing. So write and prosper! ☺

To Reneé Bissmeyer, Diana Newcomer, and my mother—Pat Isley—thank you for your dedication to this novella. And Karla Hanns, thank you for jumping in at the last minute to help finalize the manuscript.

And, as always, Janet Murphy...you rock! Much appreciation for everything you do to keep me on an even keel, as marketing guru, research aide, assistant, voice of reason, and way too much to list here.

To Wiseman's Warriors—much thanks to all of you for continuing to promote Beth Wiseman books. I'm blessed to have such an amazing street team, and I hope we'll all be on this journey for many years.

If I've forgotten anyone (and it's happened), please know that it takes a team to publish a work of fiction that entertains and inspires. I hope I've done that with this project, and I'm deeply grateful to everyone involved.

To my heavenly Father. Thanks and praise for all that You are in my life and for blessing me beyond my wildest dreams.

Made in the USA
Columbia, SC
29 April 2019